THE 23RD DREAM

Southwest Life and Letters

A series designed to
publish outstanding new
fiction and nonfiction
about Texas and the
American Southwest and
to present classic works
of the region in handsome
new editions.

General Editors:
Kathryn Lang, Southern
Methodist University Press;
Tom Pilkington, Tarleton
State University.

A NOVEL BY KATHLYN WHITSITT EGBERT

THE 23RD DREAM

SOUTHERN METHODIST UNIVERSITY PRESS : DALLAS

This novel is a work of fiction.
Names, characters, places, and incidents
are either the product of the author's
imagination or are used fictitiously.

Requests for permission to reproduce material
from this work should be sent to:

Permissions
Southern Methodist University Press
Box 415
Dallas, Texas 75275

Design by Molly Renda
Cover art by Bonnie Melton

LIBRARY OF CONGRESS CATALOGING-IN-PUBLICATION DATA

Egbert, Kathlyn Whitsitt.
The 23rd dream : a novel / Kathlyn Whitsitt Egbert.—1st ed.
     p.   cm.   —(Southwest life and letters)
ISBN 0-87074-352-X
ISBN 0-87074-360-0 (pbk.)
1. Family—Texas—Fiction.   2. Terminally ill—Texas—Fiction.
3. Texas—Fiction.   I. Title.   II. Series.
PS3555.G2974T87   1993
813'.54—dc20   93-13796

UGx

FOR RICK

I

Even the dogs can't sleep; Marian hears their tags jingle as they scratch an imaginary flea or itchy little spot of dander. Then long moments of licking, licking, licking—mindless, fastidious, determined. Until Marian thinks she might scream.

"You . . . guys . . . STOP it," she hisses at them, throwing the pillow from Adam's side in a neat arc at the same time.

Then, in the immediate silence, she misses the companionable rustling sounds and laughs out loud at their shocked submission. That must be why Adam is so crazy about dogs— they respond. In the black abyss of this long night alone, there is some control; the darkness answers back with this friendly eagerness to please her. On this sleepless night when nothing can please her. Adam's first night in the hospital.

The house is not right without Adam in it. Even the bed is a miserable mess of damp, tangled sheets, impossibly scrambled with her tossing. Never a sound sleeper, Marian is used to resting her toes lightly on Adam's legs. She often imagines that there is a charge that passes from his peacefully sleeping form into her restless one; a peace. She thinks of it now as a blue light, an energy that actually passes from him to herself. A verse floats up from childhood Sunday school: "The virtue passed out of him."

Well, no blue light tonight. No comfort. Only the children sleep. And Sigmund and Anna, Adam's morose dachshunds. Or are they only pouting still at her rebuke? Now the old house and the long night are enemies. There are noises Marian can't remember hearing before, little pecking and groaning mysteries. Even the smell is different. Or had she only never noticed it before? The wind is a howling presence, screaming in at the southwest corner, answering in futile moans through loose windows at the back. Part of the "character" Adam thought the old brownstone had. Adam's enthusiasm for Chicago—"my kinda town" he still sings to her—is a mystery.

It must have to do with Adam's rural South Texas childhood, and his mother, Margaret. She had been their most delighted guest, loving to visit and see the sights. Since Margaret's death several years ago, Adam's father, Blake, has visited only once, and that without enthusiasm. Marian shares the taciturn old man's lack of enthusiasm now. She won't admit to being afraid to be in the house without Adam, but it certainly holds no charm for her. The sick green glow from the streetlights tells teasing lies about morning through the heavy drapes. Some small failure on her part, no doubt. Things were always coming in where she didn't want them.

When Marian was a little girl her own father called her "girlie" or "blondie," as if she didn't have a name of her own. "How's my little girlie?" Maybe a quick hug for her, then words with no love in them for her mother, and he was gone again. She can remember the stiff khaki of his pants, the ribbed undershirt outlined under his loose shirts, even the aroma of Vitalis. But she cannot quite make out his face. She wonders if she would know him if she saw him, and still carries the only picture that survived her mother's anger. Marian loved him. And she hated him. She had been free to do either without consequences.

It is odd being in this bedroom alone. Like being a little girl again and in her father's house. She tries to remember that dim time, long ago, but it is like a dream. He made her feel loved; but she can remember only the feeling, not the details. Once . . . reading a red plastic menu . . . she could barely make out a handful of words. And he said to her, "Get whatever you want, sweetheart." With her mother it had always been her duty to find what was cheapest, or quickest, or most nutritious. With her daddy, it could be whatever she wanted.

Still, he was the one who went away. He left her in little steps, so that she barely noticed. First he went away on ships—huge, loud, lumbering hulks. In time she came to think of him as a ship himself, some vague, indistinct shape on the horizon, going or coming or forever floating there on the misty horizon.

She was never sure about his last departure; they all blurred together into one composite memory, neither true nor false. Looking back, she can't remember if the pain was her own or a reflection of her mother's. It had seemed bigger than Marian at first, but she grew around it. Sealed it off, an unspoken, irrevocable decision of childhood, sacred as a blood oath. "Not an unhappy childhood, really," she'd told Adam.

No, just an unhappy child.

Her father is dead to her. Not really dead; he's still knocking around somewhere in the cosmos bothering people, she guesses. But dead to her. Death by disappearance. It seems to her as if he molested her, but now the word is ruined by the social workers. Molest meant sex. His molestation hadn't been sexual. Cerebral, maybe. Yes, "a severe case of cerebral molestation here, doctor."

And if there is a God, Marian is so angry at Him too that a relationship would be impossible. Or, at best, unpleasant. What little the Lord giveth, as far as she can tell, He taketh away too soon. If there is a God, what was He doing while the Nazis stacked twelve million people like cordwood in giant ovens? What says He about the thousands of dehydrated black bodies, abdomens bloated from starvation, desiccated and blown with the hot sands of Africa? Why do the loudest proclaimers of His own good news become easy prey to the evening news, the worst of the whoremongers they decry? If there is a God, what can He be thinking? And now, of course, why this?

"And so," Adam would tease her insomniac histrionics if he were here, "why *is* there suffering in the world, honey?" Maybe he would lift his eyebrows, hold an imaginary pen poised over the palm of his other hand to jot down the answer she and the universe had wanted for so long.

Well, they've had their losses, sure. And lightning won't strike twice in the same place. Never mind that the *Guinness Book of World Records* has a guy who's been struck seven times. No, statistically speaking, that bolt won't come again. But what if fate is like heredity? She lost a parent, Adam lost a parent, their kids lose a parent. Neat; almost Mendelian.

No, let's go with the law of averages. No one seems to know why bad things happen to good people, but they don't seem to

4

happen twice. Still, the doctor had mentioned cancer, hadn't been too reassuring. Hadn't he, in fact, looked sort of tired? Resigned? Probably he'd just had a bad day and was late to go play racquet ball. But he'd sent Adam straight to the hospital and scheduled the biopsy for morning, much faster than he'd ever moved on their various and sundry injuries and neuroticisms over the years. "Lucky for me my mother taught me always to wear clean underwear," Adam had said. Shouldn't he have resisted? Was he that scared? They could've spent the whole night speculating wildly together. She wouldn't have had to do it alone.

She and Adam had agreed they should tell the kids all about it. Except the C-word. Stephen, of course, had sniffed it out for himself, though, thank goodness for his seventeen-year-old discretion, he hadn't used it in front of the younger ones. Since it wasn't in MS-DOS, Bradley couldn't compute it anyway. And Melanie, only five, seemed to think of it as a business trip and chance to fall asleep on Mommy's bed. In any case, they are all asleep now, and Marian will just have to get through the long night alone.

Grasping at the teasing little tails of sleep is maddening, so she begins to look away when they come, accounting for every sly noise insinuating itself into the house. She gropes her way gingerly around the foot of the bed to check the little alarm clock on Adam's side, hoping for a glowing green end to the long night. Years of habit are not easily broken and it never occurs to her to roll across the vacant half of the bed to check the time. Four thirty-five. "You've made your bed," Adam always teases her insomniac pacing, "now lie in it."

She turns on the little reading lamp and is stopped by her sudden reflection in the dresser mirror, older now than she'd remembered. She doesn't think of herself as pretty. She has good clothes, knows her best colors, and is an artist with makeup. Pretty enough to worry about the flirtations of men at work and friends' husbands; old enough that grocery sacker boys look right through her.

Marian's eyes, staring out of the early-morning plainness of her face, seem idiot's eyes, blankly aware of their predicament, incapable of any resolution. Up so close they are rings of brown, gold, and green. The color of tea, Adam once told her. She'll be glad when she's finally irrevocably, irremediably old; better than these sad, daily ravages of middle age.

Worry has made her thirsty and she walks over to fill a glass with water from the tap. Sigmund and Anna follow her mournfully around, toenails clicking on the hardwood, tugging at the rugs. But why is she so afraid? These things usually work out; she tries to imagine the taste relief will have with good news from the biopsy. But the fear is stronger. "Terror of unknown etiology," she imagines the doctors diagnosing the blank stare. "Unknown etiology," just as she has seen the doctors describe Adam's fevers and weakness on his chart at the hospital. Their clinical term for "I don't know." Ah, well . . . fever of unknown etiology, then. *That* certainly can't pull the critical fibers from the tapestry of their life.

Anyway, theirs isn't a life that is so delicately balanced that one pulled thread could ruin it . . . certainly not something of "unknown etiology." Not a mathematically correct Mondrian or a fragile Wyeth, after all. There is undoubtedly some element of critical form that will correct this slow slide. Sigmund and Anna sigh and jangle their tags in sympathy.

She remembers now that she never told her boss at the museum about Adam. How can she let her know that she won't be in until tomorrow afternoon? Her mind roams desultorily around the exhibit they have been working on: "Trail of Tears: Indian Art and Artifacts." All the crucial decisions have been made; still, she'd better let Gail know what's going on. She can just leave the message on the answering machine where Gail will get it in the morning.

Passing the little utility room—Adam calls it the Futility Room—she closes the door on the mound of laundry and overflowing recycling bins. Later. Marian's little phone desk in the living room seems unreal in the odd light; even odder to be making a call at this hour. Then, once she dials the familiar number, she gets an even eerier surprise: a weird electronic squeal and then the machine plays back the messages that were already there. Marian is riveted and unable to think what to do. So easy to tap into the wrong world, hear what was never meant for your ears. Redialing, she is able to leave a message, but she cannot shake the eerie, other-worldly sensation of hearing what she had not expected to hear.

Making her way back to her bedroom in the dim light, she opens her mouth to tell Adam about the odd experience. And for a split second he is there, plainly, on the tangled bed. But in the time it takes his smiling apparition to turn to her, it is gone. Marian stands rooted to the spot by the unexpected power of the vision, the eerie electronic mistake still ringing in her ears. She shakes her head and pushes the thoughts from her mind. There are things in this world that there is no explanation for, and Marian is not inclined to persist in looking for them. She had been once, and her heart still leans toward them, but she never follows.

Once, when she was a little girl, she had seen an angel. Simple as that; she looked up and there one was. She remembers the feeling of pleasure more clearly than the angel itself;

pleasure, more than surprise. She had known it wasn't a ghost, wasn't anything like her child's mind thought a ghost would be, but a huge being of iridescent, refulgent light and brilliant colors. Her mother hadn't believed her, said that it was just her imagination and that the Bible said nothing about angels having wings anyway, and to put it out of her mind and not blaspheme. Her remonstrance made an impression on Marian in an unintended way: no wings. She hadn't told her mother it had wings. It hadn't.

Well, that angel was safely tucked away with the imaginary things of childhood now. And all the other things that could not be controlled by will and determination. Marian doesn't feed that part of herself anymore, hasn't in some time. It is too seductive and has betrayed her too many times.

Of course, there had been revenants and specters aplenty in the Hellman Center; her own and the other patients'. As they all separated from their staunch allies—alcohol and drugs of every kind—they filled the atmosphere with their phantasms. Morbid, violent scenarios left their healing nervous systems and flooded the very air.

No, no. Marian finds it works better to keep things carefully controlled, efficient. Her critics call her perfectionistic, difficult to please. Her friends call her cautious, knowing the control helps ground her moods without artificial help. Besides, her own stolid approach balances Adam's carefree one. Adam's lack of motivation makes him as easygoing and pleasant as it makes Marian frustrated and angry. It's all well and good for people like Adam to go with the flow, Marian thinks, as long as they have people like her to keep things together.

But impossible for someone like her to keep things together, she admits to herself, without the easy grace of someone like Adam.

8

．　　．　　．

This dependence on Adam—is it new or had she only never asked its name? She knows that she hates to be alone. Only shadow between bond and bondage. In the middle of this last winter the paper ran a story of a young girl abandoned in the attic of a deserted house with only a thin blanket. She had been there in the freezing room for days without food or water, finally unable to move. Her legs were so badly frostbitten that they had to be amputated at midcalf. Her rescuers said that once they wrapped her up and gave her a drink she thanked them and politely dismissed them, as if she expected to continue to lie there and wait for her mother to return.

Marian had wanted children. When they came, they brought wrenching, visceral love like none she had ever known. And they brought despair that had very nearly engulfed her—such totally dependent little beings with their tiny little requirements all set in the concrete of absolute necessity. So much of it mindless and boring. Not possible to alter the needs, she had meant only to alter her moods. The doctors had meant only to help. In the sixties, while everyone else experimented with drugs, Marian didn't even drink beer and was extra nice to policemen. Then motherhood brought a more respectable flirtation with prescription drugs that was more dangerous by far. She is free of them now, but can never forget their peace, any more than Adam and Eve could have forgotten the taste of that first apple. The trick now is to put it out of her mind by a daily act of will. The strength to do that comes, in some indefinable way, from Adam. Marriage: the killer and the cure.

Adam never questions their marriage; it is a given. Constant. She can remember other girls he dated, while they themselves were just college friends and lab partners. They were an odd couple even then: Marian, meticulous and demanding, was the best of lab partners; Adam, an undisciplined English major, the worst. Most of the girls he was involved with seemed better suited for him than Marian. And yet, there are these years, these children, between them now. And yet . . .

The windows finally grow pink with dawn and Marian opens the drapes to the coming day. It is still dark enough to return her own reflection superimposed on a pink and blue sky no artist would accept. It is her frequent thought at the museum: the truest things are never conveyed in art; they are too real, somehow beyond belief. Like the evening news, standard of reality. Did war or terrorism or the ozone layer determine even so much as a turn in her day? And she doesn't believe for a minute that bit about releasing the figure in the stone, like Michelangelo, cutting away the superfluous parts. She can only add silken feathers until the shape pleases, doesn't know the shape until she sees it.

She watches as the early-morning sky slowly turns into a blood-red flame. "Red sky at morning, sailor's warning." The thought brings her back to herself, away from the dumb animal that fear had turned her into. Time to get the kids up and start breakfast. Frying bacon—Adam calls it the "universal panacea."

The pleasure of the mundane had been her cure. The satisfaction of covering children's clean toes with smooth percale sheets still warm from the dryer; grocery store strategist, making executive decisions regarding budget, health, education and welfare. She defines herself with these things. College degree aside, at her very core is a simple streak; Adam knows it too. Once he asked her what was the highlight of her life.

"Having the babies," she had answered, too quickly.

"Having them? Or *having* them?"

"*Having* them, yes. And bringing them through all that pain into reality. And nursing them. A new thing; it wasn't *like* anything else, not like anything that had happened before. Not half of a simile." She had answered piecemeal, slowly, in case he was teasing; but no, he seemed to want to know.

When she had gone to work at the museum, it had been the mundane she had loved, even while they groomed her for the artistic and administrative. The satisfaction of a light properly placed with four tiny screws turned with just the right tool. While they praised her for something called "balance" and "critical form," she reveled in the smell of varnish, the slick clean of Formica tops newly wiped with Lysol. She had known she was an impostor, awaited the day the authorities would enter, en masse, and shout, "All right, ma'am, drop that notebook. It's over." She had heard of a doctor in the Southwest, loved by patients and colleagues alike, who had been found out after twenty-three years of faithful service. Turned out he didn't have a medical degree at all, only a long list of former aliases and fake degrees. His patients rose up and demanded his release from jail, his immediate return to his practice and responsibility for their children's lives. They wanted him *back,* medical degree or no.

And so it was at home. They had their "good" furniture and a few well-placed originals. But the real substance, to Marian, was that she managed to serve them meals from all four food groups in any given day. That the potted plants prospered, never owning a yellow leaf. That there was no black line of mildew around the tub and no dark hairs in the lavatories when company came. Even now, laying the slimy strips of bacon in the pan, she derives pleasure from arranging them in an alternating pattern—head to toe, toe to head, side by side—until they utilize every practical centimeter in the pan. She smooths the first rebellious little bubbles with the spatula.

The aroma of the bacon does its work and she can hear the children stirring upstairs. Then the tiny bear hug from behind that can only be Melanie. This is the one they hadn't really meant to have. "Change-of-life baby" her mother insists on calling her, even though Marian isn't even yet the age for that change. Marian refuses to argue with her about it. "You should only argue with reasonable people," Adam always warns her, begging her to "save herself" for him.

"Mother-r-r," Bradley whines, "Melanie's been snooping around my room again. I can't find my new airplane glue." Bradley's entrance is, by comparison, an explosion. The airplane model in question dangles helplessly from his left arm while he flails about with accusatory gestures and moans. "I can't have *anything* of my own . . . *some*body's always getting my stuff . . ." He stops and stares at them indignantly over the lopsided frames of his glasses that are clinging to his face as if by magic or the glob of adhesive tape at the right temple.

"I did *not*!" Melanie's indignation is less convincing. Her bottom lip begins to tremble as she brushes back the baby-fine fringe of her light brown hair with her forearm. It looks more like a gesture meant to fend off blows.

"Did, too . . ."

"Did *not*! Mother-r-r- . . ." Melanie steps back behind Marian to await judgment in safety.

Adam, if he were here, would break it up with a quick joke. He would tell Melanie to be nice to her brothers, remind her that if they'd been girls she wouldn't be here. The part of Marian that is irritated by Bradley's assertive behavior is small. She is glad to have someone in the family who doesn't take their cues from her. At fourteen, Bradley's only problem is a scarcity of hours in the day. A dervish, he would steal hours from their own lives if they let him.

"Let's move it, guys. I've got to get to the hospital before they take your dad into surgery. Is Stephen up yet?"

"Well, now, I wouldn't know about His Majesty," Bradley drawls, mocking his brother's slow, deliberate speech. "He was in the shower last I heard, but could've gone to sleep and drowned by now." That old mystery of the firstborn . . . even Bradley, the second son, is onto it. And jealous in his clowning way. How to explain to him that everywhere she and Stephen had been, it was a new thing, a milestone? The same mothering, passed on to Bradley in his own time, was old-hat, just the motions. With Stephen, they had found each new piece of the puzzle together. And not usually the easy way.

"Both of you get busy on this breakfast. I'll go see about Stephen." And, over her shoulder as she starts up the stairs, "Bradley, I mean it now."

"She's gotta make sure Dad flosses his teeth before surgery," Bradley confides in an over-loud whisper to Melanie.

The real gradually takes over from the hypothetical. The goals-by-objectives people have got it right, Marian thinks. If you pack in enough objectives, it almost seems as if you have a goal. And she runs lightly up the remaining stairs to encourage her oldest son to hurry, just this once, so they can get away early.

Stephen's door is closed, as usual, and Marian has to remind herself to knock. That closed door was the first of many walls that have gone up since the onset of a stormy adolescence. Stephen, being the oldest, bears more scars from her own problems years before. Still, she can't think what a seventeen-year-old could be so angry or so secretive about. That closed door represents the lost tie with her firstborn; her heart plunges through it, but she makes her fist stay and knock and wait. "Stephen, you up?"

"Yes, ma'am, be right out." No invitation to come in.

She'd always imagined that "letting go" meant letting go of the *child*, letting him be independent and all that. Now she knows better; the child will go whether you let him or not. It means letting go of your own heart's desires, your own notions of what he could or should or would. A much harder, and thankless, job. It is a constant well of sadness that this cheerful companion with the sweet countenance has substituted an obligatory squint for the genuine smile that had nourished her. Her fair-haired boy, the light brown of her own hair and Melanie's more nearly golden on him. No hint of the near-red that Bradley's auburn hair had surprised them with. Her first, the child of her heart; and so different from herself after all.

After Melanie, a hysterectomy had been necessary. For nearly a year afterward Marian had dreamed having babies; dreamed and dreamed them until she would wake too tired to put one foot in front of the other. Little nameless, faceless lumps pushed out into the sleepless night like sheep that needed counting. Or there would be a variation: months later someone let it slip that the now defunct uterus had contained a baby too small to live, but that it had indeed lived and was being raised by strangers that she, Marian, had only to confront and take back what was rightfully hers. In most of the dreams it seemed as if someone had stolen the baby, as if she had been robbed. But sometimes, too, it would be a long, black void of searching for something or someone she had simply lost, or misplaced. Only gradually, reluctantly, had time blurred the severed fulfillment. Stephen's growing independence leaves the same sort of hole in her heart.

"Just don't talk to him again until he's eighteen," Adam had suggested. He had coined these vagaries of puberty Stephen and Bradley muddled through "AD"—"Adolescent Disease" —and threatened to organize a national telethon to help stamp it out.

"Mom," Bradley is whining when she returns, "we're out of milk." He swings on the refrigerator door, staring morosely inside, hoping some might magically appear. "How are you ever going to get Mother-of-the-Year?"

"You've been drinking too much milk, Bradley."

"I can quit any time I want to," he leers at her with a dope-fiend slur.

Late now, she pulls the threads quickly together, dressing Melanie, taking a half-hearted swipe at the kitchen chaos. This is the most conspicuous moment of Adam's absence. No one bothers to unroll the morning paper lying on the table. They almost forget to take the dogs out. Sigmund and Anna are even more morose than usual, patrolling around and around, sure their beloved master will appear. Adam claims dogs are not actually idle, that each has a profession that can eventually be discerned. Sigmund and Anna, he claims, are PI's: "private investigators, putting their long, cold noses in other dogs' business." Old Molly, a brown mutt on his father's farm, had sold Avon; her sensible daughter ChaChi shows Tupperware.

No one kisses her and blithely closes the door on the morass of morning. The children are all punchy from the suspense about their father and, probably more importantly, because there are just a few days of school left. And yet there is a strand of joy, too. The pleasure of the beautiful May morning? The satisfaction of managing alone? She hasn't time to wonder; they rush headlong into the waiting day.

2

Adam's earliest memories are of the window over the kitchen sink, where his mother's back was centered. It faced north, and so came to be the orienting detail for his sense of direction in general—or, more accurately, his lack of any such sense.

He knew the window faced north because of the excitement of each "norther" he watched slam into it. There would be a distant ominous cloud on the flat South Texas horizon that swelled hourly, a certain stale stillness in the air while the breeze was undecided, then a bright rattle of dry leaves as they were sucked from the trees still harboring them as late as November or December. The first wall of colder air was usually dry and full of dirt, leaves, and scraps of paper long lost in the surrounding weeds. Sometimes, if the norther was a wet one, the drizzle would sting the windows and Adam would run outside and turn his face up and north into it until his mother or Fina, their maid, noticed.

As long as he was near enough home to figure out where

that window would be, he could figure out which way was north. The dust rolled in over the horizon, picking up momentum over the plowed fields that his father was farming and the open pasture where he kept his small cattle herd. Soon the whole quilt of parcels of land, stitched together into "La Esperanza," would be enveloped in a windy wall of dirt.

All these years later, he thinks of that window as he looks out his hospital room window high on the seventh floor into the red clouds of sunrise. He had been mistaken about his room's location; he can see that now. Marian had mentioned the hospital's southeast parking lot with a general wave of her hand, but only just now as he waits for her by the window does he realize that he had visualized it all wrong. He's facing east, not south as he had thought last night. Now that he understands where the room actually is, he feels like he's moved to a new one. It could have happened, of course, with all the rooms identical; they've just moved him and his few possessions.

Adam loves early mornings, though this one is closed in by anxiety. The city landscape wakes with sluggish hope, almost excitement, just like the farming country he grew up in. Both inspire a brisk sense of fresh beginning, free of the disappointments of evening. It feels odd to be planning anything but work at this hour. This week's deadlines and office crises pour in with a morning rush of adrenaline that displaces the cold paralysis of this new uncertainty for a moment. Turning from the window, he pulls his briefcase from the tiny closet and unlocks it as he positions it on the bedside table. The papers representing the usual pleasures and panics of the interior workings of Alpha Textbook Publishing Company are a momentary comfort.

For fourteen years he has plowed the elusive furrows of Alpha's editorial department. Helped shuffle the manuscripts of hopeful young men and women and safer older academics. Attended countless meetings trying to bring the vagaries of opinion and taste into some consensus only to dash it all with the realities of the profit picture. More like a huge casino gaming table than the precious literary rainbow he was chasing when he first went to work there those fourteen blurry years ago. He'd had dreams then, dreams just like those embedded in the countless manuscripts he represents now; but the years of pressing family responsibility and numbing corporate routine had reduced them to the necessities and then to just a job. Like everyone else's.

The stretching, yawning city before him reminds him only of work now, not dreams. He's worked all his life; mornings are for nothing else. All the mornings of his life, since he was seven years old, are tied together in that one reliable chain—work.

He can still remember that first morning when Blake had taken him to work with him in the fields and barns, the sense of energy in the household and everyone talking about the weather. A norther was coming, they said. It might even freeze by the next night. Everyone was busy wrapping pipes, banking dirt around the citrus and avocado trees. Adam had climbed up on the kitchen counter and sat there with both feet in the sink so that he could put his nose very close to the window's screen. He had his mother's little "Brownie's Feed and Seed Calendar for 1946" with its tiny little thermometer with red stuff in it to mark the temperature. He wanted to watch it go down, as he understood it must. His mother had shown him where it was on the hot, sweaty days and where it was on the cold ones. He had wanted to watch it go down, because everyone said it was going to get colder and the strange dusky purple cloud lay on the far horizon to support the rumors. He was prepared to sit there all afternoon if necessary. But his father came in for lunch and put an end to all that foolishness. The "end" he put to it was an ever-escalating daily work load. It was about then that Adam started calling his father "Blake."

He had always dreamed of telling his father he didn't want to go with him, had rehearsed the words many times in his mind, invented plausible excuses. But somehow they would never come out of his mouth at the right time. He was bound to Blake, smoldering resentments and all, by his sense of responsibility. After all, he was their only son.

"Mr. Stauffer?" A hospital attendant peeks in the door. Wearing OR greens and a paper cap he looks like a little boy in pajamas.

"Yes?" Only 6:45 by his watch; surely they don't mean to take him down for the biopsy so early.

"Time to go down." With the confirmation of identity the attendant throws the door all the way back and maneuvers a large gurney into the cramped room.

"So early? Dr. Kaestner thought maybe around 8:30 . . ."

"The case ahead of you was canceled, so your lucky number came up," he explains while he double-checks Adam's wristband identification and number against the chart. "That's you, all right. You've showered, shaved?"

"Yes."

"No jewelry on?"

"No." His wedding ring finger suddenly feels naked.

"Okay, hop aboard." He pats the narrow bed of the gurney-top, also neatly made up in OR greens.

"My wife isn't here yet," Adam begins to protest. "Well, maybe it will be better if she misses the first act." He knows she'll be upset, but feels silly to hold up the whole neat, green orchestra tuning up around him. He puts away his journal—a lifetime companion and habit—and locks his briefcase of work papers. Alpha Publishing will have to wait; that old comfortable identity will have to await the outcome of this sudden whirlwind. He slips out of his bathrobe and into the hospital's new identity—"patient." Then climbs awkwardly, obediently, onto the gurney.

"You a nurse?" Adam tries to fill the clammy silence.

"Nah," the attendant grunts as he maneuvers the unwieldy gurney. "I'm thinkin' of studyin' for it, though. Nights."

"Seems like a tough way to make a living."

"Whew, Lord, you said a mouthful there. Everybody's momma want 'em to study nursin'. But that's 'cause they don't know what it is. If they knew what it really is, they wouldn't let 'em near it."

"I expect that's right," Adam laughs. "There's a lot I don't know about medicine."

"Most folks. People just don't know. I get tickled, seein' these romantic movies and such . . . all dreamy 'bout their blood test. That's just a test for syphilis, is all it is. Stuff like that." He chuckles at his own observation, then sobers. "But it's a tough way to make a livin', you said a mouthful there." The whispering rubber wheels become quieter as the gurney picks up momentum.

Now that Adam is horizontal, gates hemming him in on the narrow cot, everything is different. The short exchanges the attendant has with other personnel have nothing to do with him. He cannot control the turns the bed takes, or the corners the attendant clips with the rubber bumpers on its sides. And at the end of the long ride he is powerless to do anything about the sudden cold of the waiting area next to the operating room. The aroma is something like the cold blood of a meat market, but Adam knows better than to go with that thought. Smells often anchor his memories, calling up the related stories like a video in his mind. Food cooking, his mother and Fina, the family maid. He can always smell the Desenex powder when characters on television take off their shoes. His father's shoes, yes. Tightly, precisely laced.

The shivering begins to feel a lot like nervous jitters, but there is no one to complain to or beg a blanket from. A frozen warrior from the North. Gilgamesh come to do battle with Evil. "My dragon," he whispers as he is finally whisked into the even colder surgical suite. His complaints are answered by the sudden black of the sodium pentothal drip.

Adam dozes and dreams. He is running, pursued by anonymous figures. He reaches his car, tumbles in and slams the door on his pursuers. But before he can escape into safety, he wakes and sees himself plainly, lying on the white bed, one arm lost in a snarl of plastic tubing. He knows he is in the hospital, and he knows why. But he returns to the frantic dream as completely as if he had never left it. Suspended between two worlds, half asleep and half awake, he cannot choose. He feels himself falling and snaps upright to save himself. The sensation and his split-second response jerk him awake. Heavy neck bandage; dull ache, dry throat. What time is it? Where's

Marian? He tries to move his head and smells the salty, cloying warmth of the pillow under his head. Then slips back.

The chase and the fear are gone now. He dreams of walking in a garden. Or, rather, he senses it is a garden, though it is hidden in a wild profusion of vines, trees, and flowers. He can see well enough for only one step at a time; by faith, another. He walks slowly through, touching the mossy greens and browns, gathering boughs of branches to his chest with both arms. There is no path that he can see, but he walks through the tangle, sure of some hidden way. For a while the smells are enough—the thick, heady aroma of evergreens and wet leaves, the light perfume of tiny wild flowers. He hears the breeze, insects, and busy little birds. There are bold hibiscus, tiny white daisies, crisp and clean and honest, then a gaudy array of blooms he cannot name. He allows himself to forget that he is dreaming, quits struggling to come back to the white world where he lies immobile.

The old hospital is loud and oppressive, the stainless steel elevator doors giving Marian, for the second time that morning, only her own unwanted reflection. Adam's floor—"7th Floor Medical/Surgical"—is the most unpleasant. Oldsters from local nursing homes dot the walls in embarrassing stages of near-undress. The odor—urine, medicine, disinfectant, God knows what else—and the litter of foreboding equipment glutting the halls shatter any semblance of rest or security. The nurses' station is buried under an avalanche of charts, papers, and IV bottles, the nurses all occupied or studiously avoiding the gaze of passersby. How could they have let Dr. Kaestner talk them into this grimy old teaching hospital instead of one of the newer private ones? Marian searches the faces of the staff doctors passing by, each with their own entourage of lesser lights. No Dr. Kaestner. She prays she hasn't missed his visit, then slows and pushes the heavy door into Adam's room.

She had expected to find Adam sitting in the chair at bedside, reading the morning paper. She couldn't, in any case, have been prepared for the white rubble of sheets and tubing that encase her husband. "Adam?" she whispers, sure she must have the wrong room. But it is Adam all right. The so-familiar head turns and lifts, sleepy blue eyes trying to focus on her.

"Hi." His voice is thick and hoarse.

Marian is able to beat past her shock to approach him. "What in the world . . ." she asks, unable to take in all the paraphernalia around his body and extract logical meaning.

"I'm all right. It was the test . . ." He tries to rub his face awake with his free right hand. "The test Dr. Kaestner told us about. They took me down early . . ." His eyes feel soggy and leaden. Focusing enough to see the fear in Marian's face, he gives her the comfort of his voice, a small pat. Then away again, this time into nothing.

Marian's senses thaw enough to examine Adam, asleep amid the hospital debris. Two bags of fluids with colored labels merge into a tangle of tubing that in turn disappears into Adam's left wrist, which is covered with what seems to Marian to be an excessive amount of adhesive tape. And he is tangled in layers of mismatched blankets under the inevitable white sheet. A chart and a large envelope of some sort lie over his extended legs, as if abandoned hurriedly. The meal tray and bedside table are scattered with syringes, bottles, the ubiquitous Dermassage, tissues, and tape.

Marian begins to breathe easier as she realizes that, of all the confusing array of articles, only the IV tubing seems to be actually connected to Adam. But then, as she reaches to smooth the covers she looks down at the left side of Adam's neck and chest area. There is a huge wad of surgical dressing plastered down as if attempting escape. The visible perimeter of skin is painted an angry shade of reddish brown. For the psychic horror it produces in Marian it could be blood, but she finally realizes it isn't; it is some sort of liquid that looks as if it has been painted on by zealous children. Pausing only to be sure Adam is sleeping, Marian turns and walks quickly out into the hall.

She leans against the wall, hugging herself with her arms, staring without seeing. Realizing she might be overreacting, she tries to reexamine all this unexpected data. Was this the "one small test" Dr. Kaestner had told them about? Or was it something more; something unexpected had come up, perhaps? She stands outside herself and looks at the situation, and herself in it, tries to make some sense out of it that is not only logical but clean of fear; some perfectly understandable reason why her Adam has been whisked away at dawn, subdued, flayed, and then dumped back in his room unattended. She wonders if, in the brilliant rattle of everyday life, she has missed a cue; if some revelatory scrap of information has been given her and lost. Confusion settles in like fog.

As if on cue Dr. Kaestner appears before her. He is a kindly-looking older man in a business suit, distinguishable from bankers and lawyers only by the charts under his arm and the flock of white attendants. "Dr. Kaestner, what in the world is going on? What . . ."

The doctor's eyes, leveled at her over the tops of gold-rimmed glasses huddled on his nose, register mild surprise and greater annoyance at her outburst in front of his official retinue. "Mrs. Stauffer," he begins, an edge of condescension in his voice, "I'm terribly sorry if we've misunderstood each other; I thought that when we discussed the possibility of a malignancy in your husband's case you understood the need for immediate biopsy. That is all that is, as you say, 'going on.'"

Marian physically backs away one faltering step and he continues in a kinder tone. "The procedure wasn't as bad as it may look to you. We did the biopsy and your husband did fine, just fine. It will just take him a while to shake off the anesthetic. But we do need to talk, you and I. Perhaps you could spare a few moments now?"

Marian nods weakly, surrendering to the paternal tone she loathes but can't resist. How can she deny the soothsayer, the dispenser of the truth about this frightening riddle? Dr. Kaestner is her only link between real life and this alien technological maze. He waves his little group on and motions her to follow him down the hall to a cubicle off the side of the nurses' station. It contains only a desk, two chairs, a telephone. And a prominently displayed box of tissues.

"The crying room, I presume."

The doctor smiles vacantly. "Sometimes."

A separate part of Marian counts the minutes—hard and long like a military offensive—that it takes him to deliver the oracle her heart has already sifted out. Five minutes. A tiny refrain of a poem sings: "Earth sighs, Time blinks its steady eyes; whole lifetimes are lost in the wake." And Marian is left with only: "The nodes indicate a malignancy—a type of lymphoma; high grade; non-Hodgkins . . ." His voice trails off as if he himself is considering the possibilities.

"Malignancy? As in cancer?" she asks.

"Yes, a type of cancer that affects the lymphatic system, and ultimately the rest of the body as well. Your husband will need to stay in the hospital for further tests—'staging,' we call it."

So, the beast has finally stepped from the shadows. Now what she wants to know is whether Adam will die. Or when. Or suffer. Or . . . But she's already learning the game. There's a correct way, a euphemism, an official version. How to get the information and still play the game? "What's the prognosis, then, Dr. Kaestner?"

"That, Mrs. Stauffer, is precisely the question that I cannot answer for you. The prognosis for this type of disease is dramatically improved over past years; there are new treatments that indicate patients' life expectancy may be increased indefinitely. But, unfortunately, the treatments are too new to have any statistically reliable remission rates."

"A guess, then, Doctor. Please, just an educated guess . . ."

"I can only give you the pluses and minuses as I see them right now. In your husband's favor is the fact that he's fairly young and in previously good health. However, the early history of elevated temperatures and the fairly diffuse node involvement indicate that his disease may have progressed to a point where the available treatment may not be able to completely eradicate all traces of the disease."

"In which case?"

"In which case the prognosis may not be as good. There are four stages, with Stage IV being the most advanced. They will do further tests to determine the stage and then the best treatment plan. But Mrs. Stauffer," he leans forward and puts his hand on her arm, "let's not play guessing games at this point. Let's just take things one at a time. First, I'll be referring the case to an oncologist on staff here . . ."

"Oncologist?"

"A cancer specialist. We have very good men on staff here."

"Then you won't be Adam's doctor anymore?"

"Well, I'll certainly be available; it will be a team approach, ultimately involving several different specialties."

"But who will be in charge?"

"In charge? Well, I don't know if that's exactly the way to put it. We see each other as associates. I suppose we'll all be in charge. In any case, we'll all be working together to see that your husband receives the best possible care."

"Fine."

"I'll be arranging the oncology consult and writing the orders for now. He should be alert by tonight and up and around by tomorrow. You may stay with him, of course, as long as you'd like." Standing, he extends a gentle handshake that is at once a gesture of sympathy and a dismissal. "Until tomorrow, Mrs. Stauffer."

Marian allows herself to be led back down the hall to Adam's bedside. Dr. Kaestner examines Adam briefly and, nodding his reassurance, strides out of the room. The heavy door hisses closed behind him, and, in the vacuum, Adam's level breathing is a roar. Marian hums to herself to drown it out. She is glad he isn't awake yet; she needs time to think. What is it she should be doing? Surely there must be some clearly defined "appropriate behavior," some logical next step. She searches the pockets of memory and habit. Nothing. The huge panorama of facts and suspicions stretches out before her, but the individual pieces will not step forward and give it meaning. She'll need help . . . Who is in charge here? But Dr. Kaestner has just told her: no one. Or everyone. It is the same.

She stands, staring and numb, thinking of things that are of no help. She tries to imagine what the children are doing right now: Melanie, skinny little elf-child, having a snack at kindergarten; Bradley in science, his favorite class, arguing with his teacher over some point he'd been researching since the day before; Stephen, his long frame slouching against the wall, silky hair glinting blonde as he turns, talking, to his friends and trying to work up the courage to walk with that cute girl he's been mooning over . . . what was her name? Cindy, yes that's it. And Adam, alone, floating in a deep narcotic dream.

Adam calls it her "inventory," this ritualistic little review of each child that is its own comfort. The gentle ebb and flow of everyday life is comforting amidst the insistent lapping of the waves of necessity and habit; she stoops to find that one perfect shell with life still in it, knowing, already, that she can't do it alone.

Her mother would come tomorrow if she called; Irene loves an emergency, is never happier than when called out to succor the bereaved and bind the brokenhearted. As long as she'll be near a TV for her soaps. She wants everyone else happy . . . as long as it doesn't cost her anything. But the children would be okay with their Grandma Irene.

Marian's mind glides cautiously around the thought of Adam's father. The mere thought of Blake Stauffer causes her to stiffen. He is an enigma, a strange and brooding man whom they all skirt during brief visits. He is where Stephen got his long, lanky frame. And brooding temperament as well? Marian had not really thought of it before. Since Blake's wife died he has been a virtual hermit on his ranch, with hired hands and animals for family. After one disastrous Christmas with the old man in their home, they had all gratefully settled on a yearly visit to his South Texas farm during the summer. But now, Marian knows, he will come.

The fog of confusion hangs more loosely about her now. Marian feels like a little girl, timid and unsure. She can barely remember her own father, yet thinks of him now. "Would it have been different, Daddy, if you'd stayed? Would I have the answers, or know where to look?" As much as she loathes the paternalistic gestures of men like Dr. Kaestner, there is in her a secret unsatisfied craving for genuine paternalism. Blake never offers, though they can count on him having an opinion when asked. Though Adam had found his father so difficult to be around that he moved over a thousand miles away to live and work, she is jealous of what they have. Adam is at least *from* somewhere—a farm in South Texas—with a father who raised him and owns land. Marian's idea of respectability all around. When asked where she herself is from, only the last cheap apartment she shared with her mother comes to mind.

Anyway, transplant or not, she shares Adam's idea of "home" now too, remembers with something akin to nostalgia the road south into the Valley, dotted with white crosses with plastic flowers: were they a Catholic idea of asking God to overlook the absence of last rites or some sort of Mexican memorial? And the bulletin board at the last pit stop, right where cowboy country began to give way to the flat Rio Grande Valley: Catfish buffet $4.95, Sheriff Billy Bob McWirter's upcoming talk on "Our Problem With Satanists" at the Assembly of God Church, and snapshots of dozens of fishing trophies and catches. Then the last, flat two hours of nothing to Blake's ranch; missing it by only a few miles would bring you right to the Rio Grande and Mexico. The talk in all the restaurants always centered on the last rainfall. Blake would know within a hundredth of an inch.

Marian loves the idea of a father who would know. An authority figure who could sift through the facts for the essential overlooked clue. An intercessor. She wonders now if Adam provides that for *their* children, or if it's maybe only a dream and such a father never really existed.

And, of course, there's her best friend, Jessica, only a half day's drive away. Childless herself, Jessie can stand outside that convoluted pit called "family" and share and hear without being consumed. Marian's mother and Blake will help her to deal with the awful fact before them, but only Jessie can help her deal with her mother and Blake. Marian laughs softly to herself at the thought and begins to melt into a normal posture. Jolly, capable Jessie will come and cheer her and know what to do.

Approaching Adam's bedside, she watches the soft, dependable rise and fall of his chest, studies with new sensitivity the familiar face, simple, innocent, appealing as a sleeping child's. She cannot think about him objectively with him like this; it would be like talking about him behind his back. With Adam not there to defend himself she cannot force herself to even consider the possibilities. So she only adjusts the hopeless covers and slips quietly out to use the phone down the hall.

The hospital rumbles through the morning like a huge, lumbering train. The noise rises in a steady crescendo, the metallic

31

sounds of doors and machinery overriding staccato voices. On his small, white island in the middle of this swirl Adam sleeps on, oblivious. The dancers spin resolutely round the sleeping prince, each one intent on his own part, the choreographer dead, or gone, or sleeping in the corner unaware.

3

Adam can no longer tell the difference; asleep or awake, there are only scenes with faceless dialogues:

"Cancer?"

"I'm afraid so."

"Ah-h-h," he says, and it is his own breath. "I'll hold that against you until my dying day."

"Dying day," they echo, tittering.

"But what about all those vitamins? And I've always worn my seat belt, stayed away from cholesterol. I don't even fly in airplanes, always have an annual physical. What about all those dead bolts I put in?"

"Dead bolts?" they echo. And chuckle. "Get it . . . dead bolts!" And the faceless mob turns and walks, chuckling, away. He hears their heels clicking down the long tile hallway, murmuring, laughing, until they are only a dim speck far away. Still the voices float back, "Get it?"

All the warnings swim in like a dreamy cloud: smoking,

drinking, electric blankets, tap water. "Life Causes Death." Maybe banana daiquiris cause cancer.

"Wait, there was something I was going to ask you," he calls out to the retreating figures.

It seems as if the tiny distant figures turn back to him. "Yes?"

"I just want to know . . ." But he cannot think what it was he had wanted to know.

It wasn't enough. Never enough.

What?

I never wrote that book, for one.

There are so many books.

What is the meaning of my life?

What is the meaning of a flower . . .

His mother used to tease him about his dreaminess; the harder he'd tried to pay attention the more he'd drifted off and missed things. When it would come to him later, like it sometimes did, she and Fina would laugh together, and Fina, lapsing into her native Spanish, would press two fingers to her forehead and smile, "*Se le prendió el foco.*" He can't recall ever thinking what it meant, but now, remembering, it comes to him. The light bulb had come on. Yes, and the *foco* just might *prende* again any minute. He would surely understand this whole mess.

That's the way he thinks of his whole life until now: little circles of light trailing through a velvet darkness. Like his boyhood bedroom at night, shafts of light from the curtained window pointing out the colored squares of his quilt, the gleam of oiled wood. He had been afraid in his room at night. The shadows were malevolent black dogs, intent on frightening and overpowering a small boy. His heart would skip and his breath come only in ragged spurts. He was so relieved when his mother would come to say good night, or later to stand in the open doorway. And then in the morning everyone would go on as if nothing had happened, Margaret and Blake silent and stoic as ever.

The diffuse light gathered around them even now in the darkness, around Marian and the children and himself. Now he doesn't have to wait, he can say to the object of his passion, "Am I hot, Marian, or what?" And the light between them swells and warms. "Yes, you're hot, Adam." She smiles and touches him with a wet index finger like a sizzling iron. They laugh and fall away into the darkness together. The darkness is always there around him, close and velvety; but he is not alone in it anymore.

Now this new terror, just when the old ones have subsided. Always a new uncertainty. Where have I gone wrong? Or are the sins of the fathers visited upon me? Maybe he will write a book: *Why Bad Things Happen To Bad People: Because They Deserve It.* But no; everyone has their sorrow. His mother had her share, each one resulting in a crocheted afghan or cross-stitched homily. And Blake compounded the stony silence with which he stalked their farm, or took Adam to the workshop and ground out a lamp or bowl or doodad his mother would have to find a use for, just something different from the utilitarian items he usually put together or repaired.

Fina, after one of the many drownings or maimings or near deaths of their barrio neighbors, would weep silently, onyx rosary beads clicking. Once Fina and her husband Raul had nearly lost their own small son to meningitis. Some time after the child's recovery, Adam noticed that Raul had a tattoo of Christ on his left forearm. The only artistic detail he remembers clearly is the huge pointy crown of thorns—more like that worn by the Statue of Liberty—that resulted in oversized droplets of blood streaming down. Or were they tears? His own stomach had turned over just to glance at it. What deal had been struck and memorialized in that garish memento? And why no picture of joy or victory or relief—some celebratory, cheery reminder? Why this grieving image of the doomed Christ to remember the saved child? Adam wanted to ask, but felt his Spanish falter and fail.

He misses the culture now, though years before he had been only too glad to leave it. He had been practically grown before he realized the true status of the many Mexican workers and neighbors at the poor little barrio near his father's farm. *Mojados,* many of them—"wetbacks" who had recently crossed the Rio Grande river illegally to begin the transformation that would result in brick homes full of teenagers in Nikes in only a generation or so. They blended quickly with the Anglo youth, only rarely attained the money and reputation of their more affluent Mexican neighbors, descendants of the big land-grant ranchers. Raul, Blake's foreman, eventually brought his wife Fina to work in the house and yard with Adam's mother. Their children and friends and other relatives became Adam's playmates. He loved the dark mysteries of their poverty and their faith.

It is a long day of dreams. Dreams and faces in too close, blood pressure cuff squeezing him awake, its rubber tubing dangling. Ice chips, then gelatin and bouillon; turning, coughing. Begging for sleep and jarred by the IV alarm, the thermometer, the whispering door, the rubber-wheeled carts made loud by their jangling contents. It occurs to him, as he watches the nurse swab his skin with alcohol to start a new IV, that they do the same when they execute condemned prisoners by lethal injection; swab their arm with alcohol. So they don't send them off to hell with an infection?

He finally masters the television control panel, so he can fill the waking moments with more busy, disinterested voices. So much of the day has turned out to have been a dream. Had he dreamed the word "cancer" as well? No. A new game. The old Adam has passed away, now all things are new. Asleep or awake, he knows he will never be the same.

4

"Hey, Grandma, watch this one!" Bradley yells as he throws himself off the diving board into an overzealous cannonball.

Irene drops her needlepoint to her lap and claps with enthusiasm. Bradley pauses only long enough to be sure of her attention, then swims underwater to where Melanie is playing. Irene tenses for the scene she is sure will follow.

"Bradley," she calls, the admonition dying in Melanie's shrieks.

"He pinched me! Grandma, tell him to stop," Melanie ejects from the shallow water of the pool steps and slaps over to King's X at her grandmother's side.

"Bradley," Irene begins again. But he is clear over on the other side by now, trying to look nonchalant leaning against the 4 × 8 "Rules" sign with the slanted "No Lifeguard On Duty" warning.

"I'll tend to him, Grandma," Stephen offers. He pulls his long, thin body up from the towel where he has been sunning and runs to the side and off into a long graceful dive to where Bradley is. Stephen's teenage awkwardness leaves him when he is around water, the nervous blur of elbows and knees all working together in rare harmony. Irene stares after him a moment and then turns to Melanie, dripping and shivering at her side.

"Come here, sweet face," she wraps a towel around her and pulls her in close to her body to warm her.

"I'll stay here with you, Grandma. I don't want to play with Bradley, he's bad." Her lip quivers in a distinct pout that is more coy than wounded.

"He is a terrible tease, isn't he? And we don't have to play with terrible teases, do we . . ." she croons to Melanie as she rocks her gently back and forth. Irene's wispy gray hair, tinted nearly to blue, frames the silent look of reprimand she shoots at Bradley with softness. Against the pink rouge of her cheeks, the bluish fringe of hair makes her a soft pastel blur in the shade of the poolside canopy.

Melanie snuggles up to her grandmother's plump shoulder. Her wet hair shades her eyes like a jaunty little cap, and Melanie stares down at the damp spots growing out of the falling drops. She feels good with her grandmother, even though she senses that she trades her mother for her; whenever Grandma Irene is there her mother is usually gone or leaving. But Grandma feels good and soft and smells like wet flowers and loves her best. "Grandma . . ."

"Um-humm . . ."

"Where's Mommy?"

"She went to the airport to pick up Jessica; then they're going to the hospital to see your Daddy."

"When will Daddy come home?"

"I don't know, darling. Soon."

"Grandma," Melanie begins again in a slow, quiet voice. Her finger traces the rivulet of water dripping down Irene's arm.

"What is it?"

"Will Daddy die?"

Irene drags her breath slowly past the knot of surprise. Leave it to Mellie! She pulls Melanie closer and doesn't answer for a long moment. All the first thoughts are the wrong ones. She knows Marian must think it's serious. She only gets invited for Christmas and emergencies. With the children out of school soon and Adam still in the hospital, Marian needed her to hold down the fort at home while she works.

"Oh, no, of course not, sweetheart. Where did you get that idea? They're going to take very good care of your Daddy. Mommy will be home soon and tell you so herself. OK?"

"OK." So simple. She hadn't expected more. "But Mommy won't want to talk about it." They sway together for a few more seconds, in their comfortable embrace, then Melanie, newly brave, scampers back to her step in the pool.

Irene leaves a part of her mind watching the blur of the three bodies she has come to defend; the rest dissolves into an angry reverie of lost and leaving men. Her own father, lost in a bottle at home, swearing he wasn't an alcoholic. Just used alcohol to "forget his problems and help him sleep." He rejected her and her mother for the dim fellowship of the bars. Then her husband, Marian's father, had preferred the sea to life with them. Why? Had he simply preferred the clean unbroken horizon to the complexity of a family? It would have been easier if he had died; his choice had been so naked there before them all those years. Surely these kids won't have to watch their father leave too?

Just as she begins gathering up towels and needlework in preparation for leaving, Marian and Jessica come through the gate.

"Hello guys!" Jessica calls to the children as she drops to a lounge chair by Irene, then leans over to give a quick hug of greeting and sympathy.

"Five minutes, kids!" Marian yells, to save them the dripping trip over.

"Well?" Irene asks.

"Well, Mother, it's not good. But I can't say how bad, yet. It's one of those deals where everybody's in charge, so nobody knows anything. The official word seems to be 'non-Hodgkins lymphoma,' for what that's worth." She leans back in the low chair, sighs, and pushes her hair back off her face with both hands. "It's hot out here! How long have you all been here?"

Irene, stuporous from the heat and still digesting Marian's report, is silent.

Jessie dives into the silent void with her cheery staccato: "Come on, guys, let's get you in out of this sun before there's brain damage . . ." and tosses off a two-finger whistle that makes Bradley whip around in sheer envy. No moans and groans of protest; they gather around Jessie and start off Pied-Piper fashion. Jessie is nearly as tall as Stephen, commanding and elegant, with nearly black hair drawn back into a bun that would be severe on anyone else. On Jessie it is comfortable and friendly like the rest of her.

Only Stephen slows his walk to Marian's. "What have they found out, Mom?"

"Could we talk about it later? I'm just beat and it's a long story. Dad's all right. You can go up and see him tonight or tomorrow after school, OK?"

"Sure . . ." and he drops back, gangly and adolescent again, to pick his way back to the car alone.

"Be sure the gate's locked, Bradley," Jessie calls over her shoulder.

Marian gladly lets Jessie siphon off the rambunctious attention of the two younger children and plods silently alongside her mother as she fishes in her purse for the keys to Adam's car; her own is in the shop. Adam's old Ford seems sad and forlorn and Marian notices for the first time his peeling bumper stickers: "My Child Is an Honor Roll Student at Lincoln Elementary," "I Love My Dachshund," with a big red heart.

Jessie bears the brunt of the children's exuberance on the ride home. She laughs out loud as the whole tumble of them go in the door. "Boy! It's always just us women left here holding the ol' bag, isn't it?" Making waving motions she shoos the children away. "Come on guys, off to your rooms now . . . we want clean, showered, dry and respectably dressed kids back here in thirty minutes. Now scram!" They respond to the friendly firmness and there is a sudden hollow calm. "Coffee, ladies?" she offers, heading toward the kitchen and motioning Marian and Irene along.

"Oh, I'll just go up and help Melanie. You two go ahead," Irene offers reluctantly. Unopposed, she follows the children upstairs. The boys' voices, Stephen's deep and slow, Bradley's squeaky with new adolescence, float down; arguing about hockey and basketball, what hockey players get out of studying the great basketball players, whether it improves their own game. It is a comfort, that argumentative drone.

Marian drops heavily into a chair at the breakfast nook. While Jessie makes coffee, humming quietly to herself, Marian looks at the little bric-a-brac on the shelves next to her: a Popsicle-stick pencil holder Melanie made in kindergarten, "World's Best Mom" and "World's Best Dad" statues, a flowerpot covered with seashells. She hasn't noticed them in years and most are collecting dust or rubber bands from the newspapers or other stray flotsam of daily life.

A photo of a younger Adam, sandy hair blowing in the wind, grins down sideways from a photo-wheel of family pictures. Marian takes it down and idly flips through it. Her own pictures show her hair still auburn, before it became subdued by streaks of gray. "We save our memories the way we want them, don't we?" she muses half-aloud. All these records here of our family life, she thinks, yet not one of Adam and me arguing, not one of Stephen's stony adolescent silence, Bradley's messy room, none of Melanie and me ragged and hollow-eyed after a long feverish night.

There had been others—Marian when she'd put on too much weight, Adam with his hair cut too short, the children caught in surprise with the slack, dull expression of the not-quite-bright. But Marian had thrown them all out. Only saved the perfect ones; no warts. This one of Adam, taken at the lake—can't even see the cancer, although its first tiny cell was probably there already. Should she just take it out too?

That is the thing no one tells you about raising children, Marian thinks, touching the faded photos and listening to the distant voices of Bradley and Melanie as they argue. That there is no way to do it perfectly, no point at which someone pronounces it a job well done. Maybe she had been too good at it, too thorough. Maybe if she hadn't had to have everything so perfect, hadn't held up before herself always the long list of awful possibilities. It was such a high price; she wonders now if it kept her from enjoying the children themselves. Knows it has ruined something with Stephen, made it too hard for his moody young mind to be comfortable, at peace. She has wasted so much of her life, or ruined it somehow. But it does no good to think about it.

"I do these bad things because of my childhood trauma," Adam often teases other people's angry condemnation. "You do them because you're bad."

Marian and Jessie sit and watch the slow bruising of the evening sky through the kitchen window. The neighborhood sounds fade with the light until the two of them sit in near-darkness and quiet. They savor what they know will be a rare moment of peace and then slam automatically, nearly word-lessly, into the preparations for the evening meal, a school night, another day.

Jessie has been there for all the crises of the last twelve years. She has helped her hammer out a new middle-aged freedom, a series of choices and adjustments about the nuts and bolts of everyday life. They decided to quit reading self-help books and try to see both sides of things, though Marian suspected that it came harder to her than it did to Jessie. The selfish motives in a giving person, the anger behind humor, the chaos that lurked behind her efforts at order. She'd had them in too-neat boxes of black and white until then. Jessie helped her sort and stack them.

The moment of peace and the busy preparations lead Marian away from the pit. "What I really want to say, Jessie," she begins slowly, "is really just 'poor me.' That's really something, isn't it, with Adam up there in the shape he's in."

"That is our nature, sweetie, and there's nothing wrong with doing it just because somebody already did." Jessie tears open a head of lettuce and rinses it while she talks.

"I figure we only think it's wrong to say 'poor me' because of B movies and crummy paperbacks. We learn to be stoic, then cry inside, 'Oh, God, why me!' but very silently lest anyone discover we're so base. Always cranking out new ideas, all the time, aren't we, when we can't even seem to grasp the oldest and most basic ones?" She never looks at Marian, but only at the salad. It is a new tone of voice for her and she wears it timidly.

"A family is such a delicate thing, Jessie. Puberty was an afternoon nap compared to growing old and now with this . . . I don't know . . ."

"Well, the truth is that the same thing'll happen whether we figure it out in advance or not, so you don't have to decide the whole fate of the world right now."

"Sorry to interrupt," Irene begins, entering the room with an armload of laundry, "but . . ." then, sensing that she really has interrupted, she begins to back away. "Shall I leave you two alone a while longer?"

"No, Mother, it's all right, come on in. Sit down. It's time I told you about Adam's reports." She tells her mother all the words—tests, prognosis, cancer, expectations, recovery—but Irene quickly sifts through them and retains the one that is larger than the rest, the bully.

"Cancer?"

"Yes, I'm afraid so. Stage IV, they say. The worst. But no one will say yet how dangerous it is, what chance he has.

And *nobody* up there guesses, they're *much* too sophisticated for that!"

They sit in silent contemplation of the facts before them, Marian studying her hands, pinching the skin of the left with the thumb and forefinger of the right. As the pinched fold sags slowly back to its original shape she thinks of her emotions, aging under daily wear and tear also, slowed by decreased turgor just like her skin. A subtle loss of resilience, unremarkable in the general order of things, but a slow sorrow to her now. The gentle, well-intentioned ministrations of her mother and Jessie are soothing but cannot replace the real resilience of youth. Things seem harder now; she needs more time to absorb them.

"You and Adam haven't been going to church anywhere, have you, honey?" Irene begins.

"Oh, Mother," Marian stops her, irritated. She hates pat answers. A friend had once urged her toward a commitment, some statement of belief, but she had only answered, "I can't believe right now, but I have the expectation of being able to believe." She really hadn't known what she meant herself and wasn't surprised that her friend was disappointed. She finds the whole question of God, religion, belief too complex at times, and yet too simplistic.

"No, I just thought maybe, well, if you would talk things through with someone, a pastor maybe . . ."

"That's what I'm doing now."

"Well, yes, but well, maybe Adam would like someone to visit him . . ."

Marian laughs, too brightly, too gaily. "Poor Adam would *really* get nervous if I called in the clergy, some kind of Protestant last rites or something!"

"Now, don't get touchy," Jessie intervenes, "your mother has a point. Just because God makes *you* nervous . . ."

"That's not it . . ."

"Sure it is. If someone told you it would help Adam for you to go to Tangiers and get a certain purple banana, then lay out in moonlight three nights and sacrifice a small animal, you'd do it. I mean if you thought it might help. But just say 'God' and watch you slam it into reverse." Jessie laughs at her own assessment.

"Well, you can always talk to him about it," Irene sums up, more cheerful now to have someone on her side.

"Yes, yes I will." But there is a dryness in her voice.

Middle age itself is dryness; that loss of turgor that her own hand reflects. As a new bride she had what Adam called a "brown thumb," quickly decimating whatever small plants they brought home or planted in flower beds. But with her first pregnancy it turned into a green one; everything living prospered under her touch. Fecundity had been an atmosphere into which everything sank and was transformed. Now, since Melanie and the hysterectomy, it seems as if everything is going brown again. Brown and dry.

"What about your job, honey?" Irene wants to have all the ducks in a row.

"Yes, I've been thinking about that. Guess I'd better talk to Gail about a leave of absence or something. I hate to lose the income right now—we don't really know what benefits Adam can expect yet—but I know he's going to need me to be here for him. It will depend on how much sick leave Adam has accrued and what the verdict on his pension plan . . . Well, it's too early for all that. He's still able to do some work that they bring him from the office, and I heard him discuss-

47

ing a computer and modem. We'll just wait and see. But I've already missed so much work that I don't think it's fair to go on without some agreement. And I can see that it will probably get worse before it gets better. If they can let me go on an indefinite leave of absence . . . or I'll just have to give notice."

"It's a shame, really; you've done so well at the museum. And I know you love your work."

Love? No, there's something about it that has rounded out their family life, but she doesn't love it. "I'm relieved, actually, Mother, if you really want to know. I'd been thinking about quitting lately."

"You have?" Jessie is frankly surprised. "I thought you were happy there."

"I have been. It's been a very satisfying experience. But sometimes I miss the old days when all I had to worry about was keeping the dogs from ruining the carpet."

"Adam and his dogs." Irene's commiseration is a long-withheld complaint. Withheld only because Adam is usually there and she doesn't offend him if she can help it.

"Mother, now don't start . . ."

"I know what you mean," Jessie diverts her. "I think that's Fred's basic criteria for successful housekeeping—no dog dumplings in the hall when he comes home. He never says anything, but it all plays out across his face in that first minute: 'Go, play bridge, have fun, read movie magazines and eat bon-bons for all I care, just please no turds in the hall when I come home from a hard day at work.' "

"Adam knows to never say a word. That's why we've been so clear on the ownership. And, really, he prefers those dogs to people."

"That Sigmund's pretty smart," Irene allows, "but Anna

can't even go get the evening paper. Another dog always beats her to it, or it's too wet for her to handle, or it's under a bush. Something."

"A loser," Jessie snickers.

"Yes, a schizophrenic street person . . . or street dog." They laugh, thinking of Adam and the fine professions he invents for dogs.

"It's been bad enough leaving them all day while I work. I don't know how we'll manage them now that I'll be gone so much later."

"Maybe you should get rid of them," Irene tries again, "now that Adam's sick. He probably won't be able to take care of them. Agnes Mayfield had hers put to sleep when Albert had his stroke. You remember them, Marian." Then, sensing the silent condemnation from the other two, she drops it and decides to go back upstairs and help the children.

"Well, it's just something to think about," Irene mutters to herself as she leaves.

"Or, we could just have HER put to sleep," Jessie whispers when Irene is gone.

"It's something to think about," Marian giggles.

5

Blake Stauffer eases his lanky frame down the sagging back steps, the vague pains of his seventy-six years slowing each step. He is glad for the diversion his protesting joints provide, allowing his mind to slide knowingly around the familiar before dealing with Marian's phone call. After the dark coolness of the house the heat of the South Texas sun is an almost palpable curtain, wavy and oppressive, relieved only by the canopy of pecan trees. He walks slowly through the familiar patches of shade, then sun, then shade again. In the solace of habit his eyes seek out the points of his spread that are visible from where he walks: the neat row of tractors and implements sitting in rusty, greasy anonymity against the shed, idle now as they are more and more these days, the uniform irrigation pipes jutting up from clumps of weeds, growing smaller as they recede in even spaces into the distance, the workshop at the end of the shed, closed and ramshackle.

It is the shop that beckons to him now. He used to make

things for his wife here—little, useful things, plain and practical. Margaret has been dead for five years, and they were married for forty-six years; yet he still feels that she has abandoned him suddenly, intentionally. He can't remember if he has worked in the shop since.

His greatest satisfaction had been making things with Adam when he was a boy. His Adam, who had left him for a different life in the city, doing work Blake does not understand. His only child, his boy, though so like the woman he'd called "wife" so many years and never really known, both of them leaving . . . And now Adam is sick. Very sick. Dying? Marian's careful voice hadn't said.

The little shop is dark and dusty, surprised by the sudden light as Blake forces the reluctant door open. He turns on the ancient fan to encourage the scanty breeze, then reaches up to twist the single bare light bulb hanging among the thick cobwebs. The light that the windows let in is an amber glow. Even the layer of grime has a beautiful sheen. The rows of metal and wooden tools and dozens of tiny jars of hardware reflect the dim light in a satisfying gleam. Everything is here, left in memorized order. He finds his way easily in the half-light, like a blind piano virtuoso. He gathers an array of hand tools and lays them in an arc on the workbench. Searching the stacks of wood takes longer; he looks for just the right piece, the one that has the right depth and width and grain and burl. Without knots that will split or disappoint. The measuring and marking take only a moment. Screwing the metal lathe plate to the traced hole markers takes longer; Blake's hands aren't as steady as they once were. Now he locks it into position on the lathe, flips on the rumbling machinery, and waits as it gains momentum. Satisfied that the sound is balanced and true he selects the first gouge and attacks the block with a vengeance an onlooker would think is angry. The first rough chips of wood fly and quickly coat Blake and the floor. He leans into it even harder, nearly vicious in his efforts to derive form from the shapeless block.

The lathe rumbles and whines with each touch and the block begins to relent under the assault. Blake pauses to check his progress, changing gouges, laying his large, leathery hands against the heat of the newly ravaged wood. The warmth gives him a calm pleasure and his fury eases back now into a steady effort, his hands and body leaning into their work in harmony. He knows his body will protest later, but now his mind is freed from its impotent circles. The effort, the heat, the roar of contact between wood, machinery, and tools, the soft spray of sawdust, drown the sorrow of speculation and regret. The block becomes a crude bowl. And still he spins it resolutely on—down past that rough point between knowing and becoming to a point of beauty and shape. It is the shaping that he loves and not the result, though the dark wood arcs its rim into a graceful curve that is beautiful. And empty.

Exhausted, Blake turns off the lathe and lets the wood spin ever more slowly down into a final whisper and then stillness. Empty of thought or intent, he turns away from his work and sinks to the floor by the bench. His stiff knees are coated with the same sawdust that pads their contact with the hard floor. And he prays. A prayer that is neither words nor tears but an expression and an acceptance. "An expression of myself," he had heard Margaret explain to Adam once, "which is, as it turns out, all we really have to express." He can see the little wry smile so clearly: the faraway twinkle and certain tuck of her chin that he had never been sure was happy. But peace does come, and with it the strength to finish.

By the time Josefina comes to find him for lunch, Blake is finished with the fine-sanding of the bowl and begins the final and most pleasurable stage—rubbing in the oil that brings the magical rings and swirls and shades of time to glow at the surface. He leans gently into this final, more delicate effort, calm now and absorbed in the satisfaction of seeing the fruits of his labor. Gradually he becomes aware that Josefina is watching him. He must tell her about Adam. "Fina," he begins, eyes and hands never leaving his work, "Marian called."

"*Sí?*" she answers, her voice as inscrutable as her dark Indian eyes and features.

"She says Adam's sick. He's in the hospital. They say it's cancer." He repeats the word "cancer" with the Spanish accent that will ensure her understanding. In the forty-some-odd years she has worked on the Stauffer farm she has come to understand English almost perfectly, but she speaks it only rarely. Blake speaks Spanish only when he isn't sure she will understand, or when, as now, it is imperative that she does.

"Cancer," she echoes back to him softly. Blake doesn't turn to face her, knowing her face will tell him nothing.

Fina keeps the fabric of daily life knitted together—cooks and cleans and tends Blake in her silent, persistent way. Her husband, Raul, is the unspoken foreman of Blake's spread, by default and seniority. They all live silently with their disappointments and maintain a businesslike relationship. Margaret and Fina had made it more like family while Adam was growing up; but now . . .

. . .

Raul's father had been one of the last of the proud *vaqueros* of the dying *patron* system on a big ranch. Raul had inherited only the many skills and proud memories from his father, much as Blake had acquired only this dusty cross between a farm and a ranch from his own. The Mexicans had no true equivalent word for "farm"; anywhere they lived away from town and raised livestock or food was a "rancho." And the Anglos hesitated to call anything "ranch" since the King Ranch and other big spreads made their own claim on the word seem grandiose. So "farm" it was.

He turned to face Fina. "No rain coming, *verdad?*"

"*No, Señor.*"

"We'll be gettin' the melons in by next week then."

"*Sí, parece que sí.*" She nods her head emphatically and crosses her strong arms across her bust. Standing with her feet spread slightly, she appears rooted to the spot, neither leaving nor lingering. Waiting. He fastens the bowl back into the lathe, snaps it on and leans heavily into it with the pad of oily sealer, expertly setting the satiny finish with the heat of the friction. Then turns the machine off and waits for it to rumble to a stop.

"You think Raul and the boys can get 'em in without me?"

Reflecting a moment, mostly to satisfy Blake of her sincerity, she nods her head again, "*Sí, como no.* My boys too. They can help."

"Tell Raul to bring the boys around this afternoon. Looks like I'll be leaving for a while."

"*Bueno. Vaya . . .* I will bring them. You go eat now."

"Yes, in a minute." He takes the bowl off the lathe and runs his fingers over it in a last check for tiny imperfections. He

54

quickly puts away the tools, then hands the finished bowl out to Fina. She takes it as easily as if they'd had an agreement already. Without waiting for a response he brushes past her, flipping off the fan as he leaves.

Blake is accustomed to being alone, but he misses the busy community that the women had made when Margaret was alive, always coming or going or stirring or clamoring. Now that time of busy richness seems only a brief interlude in a longer prevailing loneliness.

His mother had died while he was still small. And then one day, when Blake was sixteen, he had come in from the fields to find old Maria Elena, the closest matriarch, Carmen, the family cook, and an assortment of friends and neighbors gathered in the cramped kitchen mourning his father, laid out neatly on the dining room table in his only suit. The scene is preserved, whole and intact, anchored in his memory by two details: the virtuosity of Maria Elena's mourning and the hiss of the logs in the box-heater, its glow emitting a false and rare cheeriness.

Blake had never known his father—a pioneer in the truest sense of the word—to be sick a day in his life. And he could count on one hand the times that whole long winter that anyone had lit a fire for warmth. And, even though he had skirted the edges of other families' grief, he could never have been prepared for the theatrics lavished by those women on the poor, departed, most untheatrical of men. That the man in the ill-fitting suit grotesquely sleeping on the dining room table was his father was impossible enough; but the connection between his wiry, taciturn father and these wailing mourners huddled around a pot of hot coffee and plates of *pan de polvo* was even more incredible.

Blake can still hear the "*ayyyy-y-y-y*" rising and falling in a crescendo of staged grief with the return of his brothers and each new caller, led by Maria Elena and picked up in rounds by Carmen and the younger women who kept the dishes tidied and the coffee flowing. No, George Harridan Stauffer, determined pioneer to the Southwest, could not have been more heartily mourned by his own sweet wife, had she lived so long. Whether drawn by grief or the chance of a little *piquete* added to the coffee as an extra brace against the raw weather, those vigorous people that had adopted him—or had he adopted them?—carried him away in style from the prevailing dream of his lifetime—the scrubby little ranch that was forever tempted into farming by the growing irrigation system and the hardness of the dream.

By the time Blake's brothers had sold off their piece of that dream and moved on, Blake had been left with the slimmest of resources. But Margaret had come along to share his dream and they had renamed it "La Esperanza"—Hope—and stayed to wrest a hard living from the land Blake would not give up. At one time he had over a hundred acres in cotton and a small but quality herd of Santa Gertrudis cattle. But those ambitions had been for Adam and Adam was gone. Now he farms only vegetables and keeps just enough mixed cattle to justify the extra hands and equipment.

Blake strides down the long caliche driveway. Bordered only by the impossibly tall, thin palms—useless for shade—the drive radiates a merciless heat. Blake stares at the wrought iron arch at the cattle-guard turn-in. "La Esperanza," it still says, the rusty letters proud and graceful even after so many years of neglect.

"Hope," he mutters to himself. "For what? What was it we hoped for?"

"Adam, I guess." He puts his hands in his pockets and squares his body with the spot much as Fina had done. He studies the sign, which is swimming in an aura of heat waves, and muses out loud.

"Was it Adam, Margaret? Had you hoped for something else, something more? Most I ever hoped for was to keep on. If I was to hope for something now, Margaret, wonder what it'd be?"

An unexpected breeze rustles the dry skirt of dead leaves around the tops of the palms. "Seems like things are losing their center, Margaret. One day I'll look up and it'll just be me and that 'hope' sign." His hand reaches automatically for the hat that he usually wears but has forgotten; his huge hand stops and lightly brushes his close-cropped white hair before dropping to his side again.

He tries to remember how old they were—twenty? twenty-two?—when they laid their claim of hope to this flat and dusty land. Another lifetime. She a smiling girl, laughing for the babies who would come, not knowing about the many who would be lost. He a solemn boy, thin and hard, his only asset a long intimacy with this land. Where did they go? And the silent older couple, moving in grim determination around the business of daily life . . . how could they have been the same? Impossible. Impossible to think of the continuous line they must have lived through. The boy who loved a girl, the man who cleaved to his wife, who raised his boy, who tended the land . . . impossible that they were the same, that they could have melted into the bent and leathery old man he sees in the mirror every morning now.

A gust of wind whips the dust into a little cone-shaped dervish that dances across the drive and pushes the old iron sign into a reluctant moan. Blake waits for the last rusty screech to die out, then turns and begins to walk back toward the house. Turning back suddenly to his unseen audience he adds, "I did hope for one thing—for all the pieces of my life to outlive me. I had hoped to leave it like it was."

By the time Blake comes out of the house after lunch the men are in from the fields. Most are stretched out under the shade trees. Each has his face covered with a cream-colored straw hat, all with some grasp, no matter how tenuous, on the brim. Only Raul is sitting up—on the last step of the porch—with the inevitable straw hat folded expertly between the thumb and fingers of one hand. He springs lightly to his feet when Blake comes banging through the old screen door. He speaks only Spanish, and that in the narrow vocabulary of the fields.

"Mr. Blake, Fina said you wanted to see us." He stands with a lithe and easy grace, his face—not so inscrutable as his wife's—showing a shy concern for his *patron*.

"Get that tractor goin', Raul?" Blake asks, slipping easily into Spanish.

"Yes, this morning. We finished that back section."

"And the cattle?"

"Junior's spraying them now."

"He'll have to get 'em back to the other pasture. If it doesn't rain, there won't be enough grass for them out there. How many boys will you have to help with the melons next week, then?"

"Well, if Junior takes one to help with the rest of the herd, there will be five of us—seven with my boys to help a little."

Blake nods and stares vacantly for a long moment, then shifts his steady blue gaze to Raul's thoughtful dark one. "How many years we been bringing that crop in, Raul?"

"*Ay*, Mr. Blake," he smiles broadly, "too many to count."

"You ever missed one?"

"No."

"I ever missed one?"

"No."

"Well, looks like I'm going to miss this one. Can you get them in without me?"

Raul's face tries to assume a reflective expression. But it is obvious to Blake that Fina has already tipped him off and the loyalty and sympathy fly unmistakably across his face.

"Sure."

"Don't know how long I'll be gone. We'll check things out good tomorrow. And I'll set things up at the bank to pay the boys and take care of anything that comes up. Anything else?"

"That last piece of fence."

"Oh, yes. I'll bring the things in from town in the morning."

Both men become aware of the silence, dotted with the clicks and buzzes of the ever-present insects, and begin to move away. Turning as in afterthought Raul says, "I'm sorry about your boy, Mr. Blake."

"Yes."

Running the farm is only a habit with Blake now. His father had come to the Valley at the turn of the century, when the big ranchers broke up their land, sold off tracts, and put in the railway. To him it had been a dream: he had come with the hope of growing vegetables all year long—"Winter Garden" the rancher/hucksters had called it, while they fed the "homeseekers" watermelon in midwinter by the train depot. He fell in love with the already-dying dream of the big ranch communities and bought more land from the big ranchers than his luck and hard work could pay for.

After his father's death, Blake had attacked the farmland

with the fervor—sometimes desperation—of youth. That gradually gave way to an easy and expert routine. Then came the years of determination to hold it together for Adam. And Adam never came back home. So he and Margaret did it because it was the only thing they knew. He never thought of the affinity he had with this land as love. He had been to places people said they "loved": awesome mountains, crisp and invigorating; graceful hills laced with streams and lakes; beautiful rocky coasts. There was nothing about the land here to say "love" to. It was flat and dry as the taste of old age, the only water coming through a complex network of pipes and canals from the Rio Grande miles away or wrested painfully from the ground through risky, almost always salty, wells. And though he'd never exactly understood what Margaret had meant by "culture," he'd known that there wasn't any here to speak of. The things she and Adam talked about—art, music, literature, theater—were slick, stilted magazine and radio lies to him. They had no relation to the land.

When Adam had married Marian and it became clear that they would stay in the city to raise their family, he had taken Margaret to visit them. Marian took Margaret to all the places she had dreamed of all those years. Blake had spent the days, miserable and confined in their apartment, waiting only to go home. After the second visit they had agreed that Margaret should go twice a year without him. And then she had died. He still can't understand it; it had never occurred to him that she might die before him, that he would spend years wrestling with her sweet ghost, angry and guilty and angry again. He had finally tried to strip the house of her touch—the pictures and needlework and flowers of her femininity and her loneliness.

No, there was little in this land for him to love. But it was a part of him—and he of it—and it was unthinkable that he could live elsewhere. Unthinkable to be trapped indoors in the winter; unthinkable to do without the language and food and feeling of this curious no-man's-land that was as much Mexican as American; unthinkable that he be deprived of the complete and perfect and uninterrupted horizon. He could not breathe in the tall buildings of the city, became claustrophobic in the mountains, lonely and confused by the constant roar of the seashore. Infused since birth with the traces of minerals from the heavy water, breathing so many years the pollen-laden air, looking out for a lifetime on the flat sameness—he would never thrive if transplanted to another, even a kinder, soil. But still he does not think of it as love.

Evening falls in slow and steady perfection, the sun sliding down the edge of the ranch in its own time, never faltering or hesitating. There is nothing to delay it, no hill or building or tree. It has only its own bank of clouds to lend it variety or beauty or relief. And these it drags down in a blaze of oranges and yellows, relinquishing its heat only in a final, late swirl of purple. The last hot embers are sucked out of the gaping sky into a molten vortex. A small breeze sighs through, puffing on the parched land and people, extinguishing the flame completely. The land is beautiful at night, like a small child sleeping; the day has been too treacherous and busy to call beautiful, but, asleep, the grace shines through.

The people sit on their porches and fan themselves and gaze out into the sudden reprieve. Blake, too, sits on the porch and waits for the night to deepen. With supper over and Fina gone, he is utterly alone. The small house Raul and Fina live in is not visible from the house, and the only sounds that find their way this far back from the road are the occasional rumble of a truck or an airplane whining overhead. When he first hears the small, sharp whine from under the porch he thinks it must be one of these planes. But then a ragged yellow dog comes creeping out and shakes furiously.

"Hey there, ChaChi. Wondered where you'd been all day." He calls softly to her, but the dog whines and turns in tight little circles, refusing to be coaxed up onto the porch.

"What is it, girl?" And then he hears the chorus of tinier little whimpers from underneath him.

"So that's it!" He rises stiffly to go down the steps to her. "Yep, all slim and trim now, aren't you," he says as he runs a rough hand lightly over the animal's side. As he gently scratches one of the dog's floppy ears, Blake lowers himself slowly to the ground and peers into the space under the porch. In the rapidly failing light he can just make out a tangle of squirming behinds and white-tipped tails.

"How many you got there, ChaChi?" He talks in a soft, low drone as he shifts to see better. The dog lowers her belly to the ground and drags herself under to her new brood, alternately panting and whining in Blake's face and turning to nose the pups.

"Proud, huh? Well, they're fine, old girl, just fine. Maybe I'll get a good look at 'em tomorrow, huh, old girl," all the while stroking her and talking in the soothing monotone. He eases away from them and back into a sitting position. His body stiffens and he waits for it to relent a bit, enough to pull himself upright. Even as he softly curses his aging bones, he feels an easy pleasure swell as he brushes off the dirt, slightly damp and cool from underneath the porch.

6

Adam sits in a big chair by the window while the aide makes his bed. There are several small stacks of projects and paperwork from the office on the windowsill and in boxes that Marian has organized for him. But he is writing in his journal, a looseleaf section in a bulging brown notebook where he puts magazines, articles and clippings that he is reading or saving. Most of them, by now, have something to do with illness, things he runs across or friends bring him.

[ADAM'S JOURNAL]

It still feels odd not to go to work each morning; guess writing in this journal is a sort of substitute. And reading . . . "So many books, so little time!" And magazines, an endless avalanche of magazines. Is there anyone anywhere who doesn't have a newsletter now? The Aborigines probably even have their own, "Tribal Layout" or something. Who can the sociologists study now? "Desktop Publishing in the Bush," maybe. My reading taste currently is running toward the scandal sheets the auxiliary ladies bring. They should get a federal grant to study the transmission of communicable disease in hospitals via *National Enquirer*. Find out the old rag's a disease vector.

The illness and drugs have brought such exotic dreams. Pictures, really, more than dreams; no plot. The most frequent is a vision of dry, caked earth, barren. Then a metal tool that must be a plow, cutting deep furrows. The parched earth of the first scene makes my throat dry, sometimes even wakes me. The gashes cut into the earth then fill quickly with crystal clear water, blue-white, bubbling behind the disc, wanting to overrun its furrowed boundaries. It must be my chronically dry throat that causes that one; from the radiation.

I had Marian pick up some old medical reference books (once a book addict . . .). Now I can look myself up anytime I want. That will either be very helpful or I'll be dead from fear in a week:

> Merck Manual: "The hemopoietic syndrome, with anorexia, apathy, nausea and vomiting, may be maximal within 6 to 12 hr. after exposure to lower doses of radiation, at the level of perhaps 600 to 800 rad. Symptoms then subside, so that within 24 to 36 hr. after exposure the subject is asymptomatic."

Best translation so far is Dr. Cronkite's: "You can't eat, don't care, probably puke your guts up for a few hours and will generally feel like hammered dog meat." All proven true. When they told me they were going to radiate the "involved nodes," they didn't mention that ALL of mine are involved. "Mantle field radiation," the technician called it—neck, chest and groin nodes. Long mantle!

In another dream I am struggling in a gossamer web, no, not struggling, pushing at it, insistently. I think of the last litter of pups we watched old Chula deliver at the farm, their steaming, gelatinous arrival amid dark muddy green meconium and blood and water. That old mama dog, patient, perseverant, busy with the other canine business of placenta, etc. while a pup would squirm and paw at the formerly protective, now suffocating membrane. Such a thin web between life and death.

What I want is someone to sit with me in my sadness. We can throw ashes on our heads, wear sackcloth, experience the hollow agony of dying together. What I *get* is people telling me they know how I feel and it's exactly what I should expect at this stage. This stage? Expect? As if they've done this a thousand times before and I'm not really very original? Well, that is a sadness; I would at least like to give it a new twist; make my mark somehow before I go.

The glass of the hospital window is a smoky tint that, Adam supposes, is meant to keep the annoying vagaries of sun and weather out. He misses the cheerful dappling from the leaves outside his own study window at home, guesses "solariums" in hospitals went out with high-button boots, or central air conditioning. In any case, there is nowhere to enjoy the actual warmth of the sun or the invisible caress of a breeze. If visualization healing works, why not visualize a healing sun and breeze? It's easier than imagining tiny men with hard hats and chisels coursing through his body, destroying the "bad" cancer cells and nourishing the "good" normal cells. The many "get well" articles friends bring him are going to turn him into a neurotic humanist, he's afraid, before they make him well. "He had a very optimistic cancer right up until he died," they'll say.

The tiny table in front of him is scattered with folders, pens, and papers that Marian has brought from his office. He has managed to keep his share in the wheels of Alpha Textbook Publishing turning even though he has been too sick from both the cancer and the treatment to go in to the office. It amazes Adam still how fast a simple biopsy turned into surgery and radiation and aggressive chemotherapy with drugs so powerful that more treatments are necessary to cure the effects of those treatments. And now his sick leave is used up. He is trying to stay on regular salary as long as they will let him, but it is getting increasingly difficult to keep up. Today it is impossible to concentrate; he mostly stares out the window, writes in his own journal, and waits for Marian. She herself is talking of quitting her job soon. What then? But he cannot make his mind focus. The window draws him away from their current financial disaster to the more universal one below.

He can just make out the activities of the rear courtyard, busy with hospital traffic. Varied levels of other rooftops and vent pipes make a sort of lopsided amphitheater. "NOW SHOWING," Adam imagines the flashing marquee, "Death, Destruction & Dismemberment." The smiling people wheeled out reasonably healed or holding new infants are not visible from here. They go out a tree-lined drive in front, waved out by cheery administration people who hand them an opinion card and release slip. The entrance/exit area Adam is watching handles the other traffic: truckloads of supplies to be gobbled by the voracious monster and reappear as empty cardboard boxes flattened and stacked by furtive maids and janitors who take the opportunity for a quick smoke, maintenance men carrying in and out the tools and machinery of their trade, doctors darting in and out incognito.

Adam keeps a silent tally of one other type of traffic—this is where the bodies, the system failures, are shunted out via ambulances and hearses from various funeral homes. An odd ecology that takes in so much and gives out only these discreetly draped forms. Two so far today, only one day before yesterday . . . looking at a good week, bringing it all in for well under ten. He tries to imagine the body itself each time, inventing a scenario of death. He knows some must be tragically young, some the victims of sudden accidents, some disfigured by disease or trauma. But he can only picture them elderly and serene. Asleep.

The aide does the bed and cleans up at a snail's pace, catching a few scenes of whatever soap opera is on the television. Adam prefers the silent drama that unfolds in the loading bay below him, follows each victim's imagined journey to an elegant funeral parlor, the crying loved ones who will meet them there. He tries to conjure up a variety of different services but can only really see one, a combination of the few he has attended and the terse cowboy rituals from TV: "I am the resurrection and the life . . ." He knows there surely must be others—gaudier, louder, different.

Back home in South Texas there had been two cemeteries: "Roselawn" for the White-Anglo-Saxon-Protestant regulars (and Catholics of the right sort) and "La Piedad" for the rest (surely all Catholic judging from the garish statues, nearly all Mexican judging from the named stones). Those "resting" at Roselawn had done so in neat, orderly rows of simple white crosses and gray marble markers. Only new resting places had anything beyond a puritanical arrangement of discreet bouquets and wreaths. As soon as the grass subdued the spot, even those submitted to discretion and good taste. Adam remembers visiting his mother's simple grave; every time he became more familiar with her neighbors immortalized in white marble, pink granite, and brass plaques. It got to be like seeing old friends. But friends, come to think of it, whom he had never met.

"La Piedad," on the other hand, had either never known the rules or had its own. Adam smiles even now to remember the wild profusion of plastic wreaths and ornaments trailing yards of shiny ribbon. Crumbling plaster saints mingled with towering whitewashed Marys and crucifixes tipping under the weight of their bloody burden. He had always been spellbound by the statues of Jesus opening his own thoracic cavity to reveal a gaudy painted heart dripping both its own blood and a sort of ray that he supposed represented glory.

Adam sees himself, neatly sleeping like those forms leaving below him now, arriving at the center of town in his own hearse. They are at a loss as to where to inter Adam Stauffer: not exactly Protestant (would the neat rows at Roselawn blackball him?), not exactly Catholic (would they be any the wiser in that wild chaos?), and not exactly Jewish (where were they buried?). The man without a country. "Here I stand," Martin Luther said, "I cannot do otherwise. God help me. Amen." Yes.

"Adam?" Marian's staccato greeting snaps him back from the reverie. Doesn't Marian's voice seem sharper these days? Almost as if she's angry at something.

"Adam, what have you done to your hair? What happened?" She reaches out as if to touch his head, thinks better of it and lets her hand drop. As if to complete the aborted thought for her, he reaches up and ruffles the stubby patches of hair left on his now nearly bald head.

"It was falling out Marian. I would have been bald soon anyway. So I just cut it off myself. Wasn't about to get cheated out of even that; just sit idly by and watch my own hair fall out. After all . . ." But he won't look at her. He sounds apologetic, like a naughty child. "Anyway, I kind of like it!" grinning up at her, trying to buy back some leverage.

"Well, yes," she agrees, too quickly, "it does suit you, somehow; sort of boot camp macho." She busies herself around the room, tidying the paper and plastic chaos that has crept in during the night. "Actually, it's not so avant-garde as you might think. Have you checked your neighbors out lately? Looks like you all share a psychotic barber. And you can't really say Dr. Yee didn't warn us." She stops behind his chair and cradles his tufted head between her breasts, hugging him to her and swaying almost imperceptibly a moment, as if rocking a child. "Besides," she whispers, "it will grow back thicker, they say . . ." His cheek seems tan and leathery in comparison to the pale, virgin scalp. If she could see his face, if she dared to move around and look in it, she knows she would see the fear. She has seen it growing there these last few weeks, though no one names it. His eyelids, closed now against the light or against his own tears, would be pale from the anemia, nearly colorless. But she will not look.

The first few weeks at home had been fine, Adam almost his old self, Marian limp with relief, the children assuming the best. Even Blake had been pleasant. So out-of-place and restless, he had nevertheless taken a special interest in the boys and been available to stay when she'd had to run errands or tie up loose ends at work. He and Irene had only bewildered each other, as always, and Irene had responded by going back home to Smithville to wait until she was "needed." Adam had worked some, but it quickly became apparent he would have to go on a medical leave of absence. He and Blake seemed to enjoy each other's company and Marian wondered if the relationship was new or if she herself had hindered it in some way before. Even Stephen seemed drawn to the taciturn old man and included him in his secret world. Marian had been sad—or jealous?—to hear them arguing over Stephen's books:

"But have you ever really read Gibran's books, Granddad?"

"Well, sure, son. Your Grandma Maggie had that one. Never cared for it myself, but guess it'd be okay for someone who couldn't take their Bible straight yet."

Couldn't Margaret? Marian wondered. But Stephen didn't argue or seem offended at the ruthless arrogance of old age. He had, in fact, been the only one to tag along when Blake went to church on Sundays. Bradley was somewhat taken with the old man, his quaint ways, acerbic manner, and especially with his skill with hand tools. But not enough to go to church and risk cramping his own style.

Marian was embarrassed by the sudden interest in spiritual things, but even she had made a short, faltering quest those first weeks when she had taken her mother home. It was only a comfortable two-hour drive east, so she had spent an hour driving around the small town. Unable to conjure up any feelings she would admit were nostalgic, she nevertheless ended up pulling into the parking lot of the little Methodist church of her childhood. The memory was clear, of being here with her grandparents and her mother, but there were no feelings attached to it. Marian thought she should feel pleasure or regret or something. Everything was as it had been, only painted over (probably many times by now) and padded with a few luxuries that were new: cushions on the pews, carpet in the aisle. Without meaning to she had found herself asking for the pastor in the little office. She can't say even now exactly what it was she had wanted, what she had hoped to find. Gaudy saints, maybe, or icons like she had seen in cathedrals, things with names and specific purposes one could invoke in times of need. Or even swelling organ music. Instead there had been a young man in a trim dark beard and neat blue jeans who was "into" TA and motorcycles. Her halting questions had died on her lips.

"I hate myself for these feelings," she had cried to Jessie. "So angry, so critical. I'm certainly keeping them to myself, not harming anyone with them. But still, if I could just keep that one part of my life clean now, pure . . . With everything else so chaotic, it would help if I just didn't want things I can't believe."

"You can't believe?"

"No."

"But you want to?"

"Exactly. For more than just comfort. If there were hope or help for Adam, I would ask for it."

"Can't you just ask for it whether you know what's there

or not? There will be things you both need besides healing."

"No. If there's no answer, I don't want to know. The silence, the wrong answer, either would be more than I can bear."

"What does Adam say?"

"For starters, that there's worse things than dying."

"Well, yes. And Marian, please be easy on yourself. Don't hold yourself responsible for everything. When you get to where any emotion is abnormal, you'll crack."

"It's just that I don't even know who I would be without Adam."

Now, with Adam back in the hospital again, things are easier for her. "I'm trying to be easier on myself now, Adam," she whispers into his neck, still swaying gently. "I wish you would do the same."

"Listen, Marian," he says, patting her arm as his voice shifts gears into a cheery high, "Dr. Hohner was just by; flattering my white corpuscles again. Meaning we're on track with the chemo." More than just a progress report, it is a deliberate change of topic.

"Oh?" Guarded, unconvinced that this is a complete report.

"You know, I think I've figured out the problem with the practice of medicine; what do they call it now? The 'health care delivery system.' Jeez, what a system."

"I figured you could do it if we just left you alone up here long enough with time on your hands. Shall I call for a press conference?"

"Not yet; I'm still formulating a concise theory. Besides, there's the research grants to consider; have to let the ol' boys down easy. Wean 'em from the government tit, as Blake would say."

"So, what is it, Adam?"

"It's too specialized; just like the rest of life, everything's too compartmentalized." He wants to tell her about the odd traffic in the courtyard below, but knows it would result in a room change. "People just can't see the whole of a thing anymore; they're separated from the consequences of their actions. And that's dangerous in medicine. Seems like most around here care a decent amount about their own little part insofar as it keeps people from croaking on their shift. But they don't have to look at the results others reap."

"I'm not following you, Adam. Probably because you aren't telling the details. What's really happened?"

"I've been interviewing student nurses, and . . ."

"I knew it! Adam, you're going to have to leave those poor girls alone. They probably think you're a faculty spy."

". . . and they were telling me what all they have to do to a body right after a patient dies: close the eyes, align the jaw and limbs, pack the rectum, take the paraphernalia out from all orifices. And the whole time I was thinking that they were not the ones who had taken care of the live person. It wasn't so long ago that families laid out their dead on the dining room table while the women bathed and dressed it. Now fourteen people have a little piece of the whole guy, then when he croaks some nineteen-year-old girl who never knew him comes and shuts him down."

"Now, Adam . . ."

"And then a couple of boys not much older than Stephen come in with a tasteful stainless steel cart on whisper rubber wheels and carry off the evidence. Nothing to anybody except whoever's shift it happens to be; and they swear they did their little part one hundred percent."

"I know what you mean, but I don't think it helps you to be so morbid . . ."

"Like the Joads."

"The Joads?"

"Yeah, you remember. *Grapes of Wrath*. Separated from the product of their hands, the fruit of their labors."

"Oh, yes."

"And the astronauts."

"Separated? . . ."

"No, no, not that. The ones that blew up because of a faulty O ring. Do you suppose the guys that made and tested that rubber ring ever saw those mangled bodies after they finally recovered them from the ocean floor? They most assuredly did not."

"Well, that's science or technology, something else. These are the 'helping professions.' "

"Kill you or cure you."

"Adam . . ."

"I've been reading medical journals all afternoon. Do you realize that the AMA hasn't even made up its mind if circumcision is beneficial or harmful? Thousands of years rabbis been lopping 'em off and these ol' boys are still sitting around long tables talking it over."

The lurking aide is ready to put Adam back to bed now and they are both relieved to have the tangle of intravenous fluids and poles and tubing to wrestle. Anything to avoid faces. There is no need to respond now and they are both more comfortable with the alien technology than their own thoughts and feelings. That clinical onslaught has become their friend, separating them from the need for an intimacy they aren't ready for. They had argued about it at home:

"Marian, I can bathe myself, don't worry about it."

"But it's been days since you were able to get down into the tub and have a really good bath. You need a good warm soak; it'll help the bruises heal and maybe I can get most of the tape mess off."

"No."

"Adam, why? Let me help you."

"I don't *want* you to help me. Try to understand, Marian. I can't work anymore, can't even finish the stupid little projects they were willing to let me do from home. Can't drive, can't fish, can't go to parties. All the pieces that really made up my life are slipping away. I know it sounds silly, but washing and trimming and picking and peeling and wiping this old bod was important to me; I probably spent a third of my life tending to it. And I'm not ready to give it up yet." And, the clown peeking out around the sad facts: "Personal Hygiene Is Sacred. Got it? When I can't keep the big pieces cleaned up I'll get a nurse."

"You'd get a nurse with a perfectly good wife standing here?" she had pretended great offense. "Adam, is there something I don't know about that bod you're so private with all of a sudden?"

They had both laughed about it then, but Marian knows he's serious. She thinks now that's why he was so willing to come back into the hospital. He had seemed relieved when it became necessary to have transfusions and further testing. She can see now that he prefers to have his physical needs met by the staff. "Ya seen one, ya seen 'em all, Mistuh Stauffer," the first black aide had told him as he'd vigorously scrubbed things Adam had forgotten he had. Funny that Adam would avoid this intimacy with her now when he'd always been the one to seek it before.

It was always Adam who "accidentally" left on closet lights,

75

"forgot" to close the drapes when he sought her those tender nights. Adam who appreciated touches she would have found embarrassing. And, through the bloody, milky, messy business of three babies he had sought her with even more eagerness, almost an animal delight in the dripping female weight of her. Odd that he could not now let her simply bathe him.

"Dr. Kline says I can go home in a few days. My blood count's up and the scan didn't look too bad."

Marian lets the "too bad" slide. She can find Dr. Kline later and get a full report. "That's wonderful! The kids will be happy. Your Dad too."

"How is *that* turning out?"

"You'd be surprised. The boys are actually enjoying Blake for a change. He and Melanie and I don't much know what to make of each other, but we're doing fine." She can tell Adam is relieved. "He says he's going back home soon but seems to really be counting on our visiting there when we can."

"Yes. Maybe this summer when the kids get out of school." His voice is drowsy; he usually sleeps after the morning ritual. Marian pulls her chair close to the bed, sits down, and takes out a bright roll of needlework, her newfound solace. Adam watches her careful stitches with a sleepy curiosity, then lies back and closes his eyes. "Marian," he murmurs in a sleepy drone, "they wanted to know if we wanted to freeze some sperm." A tiny grin peeks from the corners of his slackening lips.

"What?" She leans toward him, thinking she has surely misunderstood.

"Yeah. My sperm. Some guy came around from the laboratory. Said the doctors routinely have 'em check with the male patients about to undergo extensive radiation to that area.

76

Seems they can save your sperm for several years in case the radiation leaves you infertile."

"Weird."

"Really. Some kind of immortality, huh? I've thought of some things I would like to preserve from my lifetime, but I hadn't thought of that one. They said it was just a routine question. Imagine. Some routine, huh?" He is drowsier now, and only murmurs softly and keeps his eyes closed.

"So what did you tell them?"

"I told them you'd had me fixed years ago so I'd stay home nights."

7

Dear Jessie,

Our phone bill this month was outrageous so will try putting pen to paper. Hope you and yours are well and happy. We all miss you around here and are eagerly awaiting your visit. Mother's here to help with the kids and Blake's gone home, so it will be a good time.

There's no sense dreaming up stuff to fill this paper when we all have the same thing on our minds: Adam. We had a fairly pleasant few weeks at home since his last hospitalization but I'm afraid we're back now: Med/Surg room #542. Adam says he always wanted us to have a second home. Seriously, though, he is worse. The doctors are not so optimistic anymore.

Stephen is taking drivers ed and Adam was able to go with him a few times. Said his new hair will probably come in white now. How the children do stare; say nothing and stare. We talk some, but they're more into the avoidance mode. Adam keeps up his humor, but I don't see how. Like most clowns, there's an angry boy underneath.

This hospital is a nightmare, but it's getting to where I prefer it to home. At least there are people to check my thoughts with. And you know how Adam is about me "nursing" him much. Speaking of which, here comes his favorite. Better run.

In her haste to fold the letter, seal it, and slip it into her bag, Marian forgets to sign it. She greets the day nurse—"Angela West, RN," the gold nametag gleams—and pats Adam gently awake. He wakes with a start, swearing he hasn't been asleep, only resting his eyes. Clearing the books and magazines away, Marian gathers the scraps of paper where Adam has scrawled various quotes. "You will be dead so long as you refuse to die—George McDonald" ends up on top and she deftly slips it into his bulky journal. As the nurse begins the daily ritual, Marian sinks back down to her chair and picks up the needle-work. The nurses have hinted that many spouses help the patients with their personal care. But Marian never offers and they don't insist.

Marian can't use this opportunity to go for coffee because the doctors are due on rounds. "Sentinels to the Sick," Jessie calls the relatives waiting in the elaborate ritual of physician-trapping. Outside the operating room and intensive care units, which have no rear exits, the ritual is an art form. Warned by the nurses—whose side are they on?—the relatives swarm to the doors. There the besieged physicians are forced to dispense crumbs of hope or doom, like cornered movie stars signing autographs. Here in the rooms it is a quieter but more arduous task, often ending in a bitter defeat. But Marian intends to stay and try.

Marian has learned the system well, only failing when some invisible crisis deep in the bowels of the hospital short-circuits the route of the physicians themselves. She herself never misses a beat. Waiting is her game now. A lady-in-waiting, waiting on the Lord, waiting in line, waiting in season and out of season, Waiting for Godot. Then she shuffles these together and deals herself a new hand, but always of more varieties of waiting. She has added handwork to her routine, trying her hand at knitting now. Knit, purl, knit, purl; the hypnotic regularity soothes her.

She wonders when deity was conferred on these men of medicine; confirms it daily herself. How did the primitive mind endow the attributes of deity on the leaping medicine men? Or is it a modern twist? After all, it wasn't so long ago that barbers practiced medicine.

Something in Adam's voice draws her attention. She notices a new plaintive quality as he argues something with the nurse, almost whining. It embarrasses Marian, but the nurse, if she notices, doesn't let on.

"But she's so rude," Adam complains. Miss West seems unmoved.

"She may seem rude at times, Mr. Stauffer, but guess who *I'd* want on my side in a pinch? There's really two kinds of nurses, the way I see it: handholders and lifesavers. Right now you want a handholder. That's me." Her rueful smile turns a businesslike face pretty for a moment. "But the day may come when you'll need one with her skills. I've seen her pick dead people up by their pajama-fronts, throw them on the floor and *force* them to live again. Resuscitation takes on a whole new meaning. They taught me those same basic skills, but she's doing them while I'm still trying to find the crash cart."

"Maybe so . . ." Adam acquiesces but does not seem convinced.

"Of course, the patient may not even remember all the commotion . . . and wants me when he wakes up from it all!"

Most of the people who care for Adam, including Angela West, RN, give the impression they have never been sick a day in their lives. It seems almost ghoulish to Marian that they are so willing to discuss their trade with its victims. Like the TV special that taped an interview with an imprisoned child molester/murderer that showed him plainly boasting of his skill at enticement. So many strange contradictions in such a macabre business. The "health industry" they call it. Some industry; and no health.

Marian has taken to playing "adjectives" lately; a sort of game of clinical shorthand. Adam's "bad" today and she's "scared." She's trying to whittle things down to where they don't need adverbs. Is he "pretty" bad or "real" bad? Is she "almost" scared or "real" scared? Adam is "brittle," then. Crying easily, euphoric sometimes, shaky. Something to do with his blood gases they say. Surely there's nothing wrong with her blood gases, though, and she feels very nearly the same way. And she is "frozen." Just past something one could lightly call fear.

So far today there's been nothing she could do for him but wait to talk to the doctor. And nothing the doctors could do for him but send in another doctor. So she has expanded her waiting program exponentially, with elaborate checks and balances to be sure she doesn't miss that critical detail she's been afraid of missing all her life.

"Adam, just try to lie back now and take a little nap." She smooths the frantic covers and urges him back. His nurse is gone but he continues to ramble on and on about the rest of the staff. He is not quite lucid, but not quite incoherent either. "It just hasn't been a very good day; but the doctor will be here soon and give you something to help settle you down."

Unexpectedly he looks her straight in the eyes. The cloudy blue of his eyes is ringed now by red, giving him the rheumy stare of a drunk. Some fuzz—he won't call it hair yet—has grown back in, a little halo against the bright fluorescent lights behind him. "I can always just give up. You have to keep on keepin' on. And I'm no hero, Marian. I have every intention of giving up if the going gets rough . . . if it gets rougher . . ." and, starting to cry, "maybe I've given up already . . ."

Marian is paralyzed by the sight of Adam's tears. But he stops them and the old Adam peeks around their dampness still clinging to the scant lashes: "Sometimes I think I should have gone off to eat peach pits in Mexico or something."

They are the last words she is to hear him speak for a long time. He looks at her, frantic, surprised, clutching desperately at his chest. He mouths the words "help me" and what she later thinks must have been "I can't breathe." By then she is already in the doorway getting help. The rest is a blur that she cannot digest, that later she will not even be able to remember clearly. "Organized violence," she thinks. There are suddenly several white figures hovering, yelling, pushing, slapping. Electronic monsters are brought in to add to the chaos, blinking and buzzing lest any space of sight or sound be left

unfilled. Modesty and dignity are cast aside with the interfering linens and Adam's nearly nude body is laid out in mute submission.

There would be no way to approach his bedside now, even if she had the strength of will; every inch of perimeter is occupied by frenetic, scowling figures in white. Marian feels as if they are using up the little oxygen left in the air, that any moment the tiny scarce molecules will have been sucked in and she will sink, limp as a rag doll, to the shiny linoleum.

But before that can happen someone notices her, a clammy statue near the door, and gently propels her to a chair in the hallway outside. A throne where she must rule and reign even as she dies for want of air. Respiratory failure, they tell her. Something about the tumors dissolving and overwhelming the lungs. Does she want him put on a respirator? Will she sign for it? Does she understand the procedure, the risk? No, without it there is no hope. Well, then . . . Not willing to be left with "no hope" she signs the papers waving in front of her, gasping, wringing her hands together while they read them to her. She signs for "cut-downs" and "CVP's" and other cryptic ways for the doctors to cut into her Adam's veins and arteries, trying to save his life.

Then they are all gone, a frenetic parade, bearing her Adam along, bed and all, banners of bloody linens unfurled and trailing a brutal and telltale debris. That odd spasm of his naked foot, what does it mean? Is it the last life left in or the last gone out? Even the quick cursory glance at Adam she allows herself tells her not to look again and she wanders back into the vacant room.

It seems cavernous now, as if enlarged by the horrific storm that sucked Adam away bed and all. She'd have preferred a

whimper, not this bang. Was the world ended? There were no guarantees and all the soothsayers had scurried out alongside Adam, the sleeping prince. She wanders aimlessly in the room, wondering at the discarded needles, tubing, dressings, and instruments strewn everywhere. If these were the ones that had missed their mark, how many must now be hanging from Adam like so many tenuous arrows?

"Mrs. Stauffer?"

"Yes?"

"They are taking your husband to have a lung scan down in radiology, then they will put him into the intensive care unit on fourth floor. I'm afraid you can't go with him either place, so you probably won't be able to see him for a couple of hours."

"Oh . . ." Not comprehending, unable to move. Is this person a doctor? A nurse? The janitor? Who knows . . .

"The doctor will give you a report after they install him in ICU." Install him? Like a new dishwasher? Has he passed that fine line between humanity and machinery? "They'll look for you in the waiting area outside ICU in an hour or so, if you'd care to wait there . . ." He gives her an opportunity to respond, but when she doesn't, begins to clean up the room. "We'll be putting someone else in this room as soon as we get it cleaned up. Would you care to take his personal things along now or shall we hold them for you to pick up later at the nurses' station?"

It begins to dawn on Marian that she is being evicted from this room, their "second home" that she has managed to feather into a sort of nest for them in spite of the obstacles. Moved unwillingly to the next act of a play she'd never auditioned for. If an actor dropped dead onto the stage between

84

urtains, would they just carry him stiffly offstage before the next scene?

Other actors drift in and out, some offering faint words of comfort or encouragement. The end result is Marian standing alone in the elevator holding a paper grocery sack full of her domestic instincts and Adam's soiled pajamas. She can't remember what floor ICU is on, doesn't want to go there anyway. So she rides along with the stream of traffic, finally exiting on the ground floor. She feels helpless, wandering the halls with a paper sack of dirty pajamas, not knowing if their owner is alive or dead. Not even able to find out. There is no one to offer explanations, no one to make it be all right. It is as alone as she has ever felt. Even paternalistic, condescending Dr. Kaestner would be welcome right now. She had worried about every inch of Adam's body and every obscure place the malignant cells had shown up. Except his lungs. She had not worried about his lungs. And they have ambushed them in this unlikely way. She would not neglect any unlikely detail again. She would worry faithfully about everything.

8

A large bouquet of flowers in a heavy marble vase catches Marian's eye. There is a burnished brass plaque on the door next to it: "CHAPEL." And in smaller letters: "Open to the public. Chaplain's hours 10:00–4:00." Just seeing the hours listed there compels her to check her watch. Two thirty-five. The idea that she is somewhere and that the hours are right makes her want to go in. She is the public, after all, and it is between ten and four. There is meaning. And order.

In the tiny foyer is a small table with a simple brass cross beside an open "Guest Registry." The varied flourishes of handwriting are irresistible. Marian is drawn to the open entries, reads them with an embarrassed sense of intimacy, as if she had come across an open diary. People from all over the country have signed their names and given their addresses. Many have written notes under "comments." Most offer simple thanks, to God for granting some request or to the chaplain for providing the serene place of escape.

Running a close second are those begging God or some in-

determinate audience to resolve a conflict, burden or tragedy: "Please pray for me" or "for us." Some include words in quotes; too rich for this traffic of humanity, they must be scripture quoted to apply to the need. "Be ye not conformed to this world, but be ye transformed by the renewing of your minds" and the most popular: "All things work together for good to them that love God." Some merely note the verse they want to waft before the noses of the curious public: "John 3:16" is a favorite and Marian remembers it from childhood Sunday school lessons. The others are familiar, too, though probably, she suspects, from roadside signs and cross-stitched homilies. The bits of secular wisdom are prevalent too: "Be careful what you believe," one warns, "it may be true."

Marian is fascinated; the rough scrawls and prim cursives reveal the individuals who had entered them. She wants to add something herself, leave some marker of having passed this way. But the paper sack she is carrying is clumsy and she passes on into the little chapel: six or eight rows of pews and a tiny altar. It is dim and her eyes adjust slowly from the glare of the hallway.

The interior is only vaguely ecclesiastical—pews of burnished wood, green velvet cushions at the altar. The crucifix is not repeated here; no offense to any denomination. Marian at last is able to put down her burden of bags and purse. Seeing no one but a child humming gaily to herself on the front pew, she exhales slowly and sinks down to the cool wooden bench, lets her tightly held arms and legs and abdominal muscles go loose. Her hands brush the invisible refuse of the day back from her face and toy hopelessly with her hair, then they too become quiet.

She can only dimly make out the noises from the hallway outside, and in here the only sound is the rush of cool air from the air conditioner vents and the sweet humming of the child, giving the dim room the air of a monastery with distant chants and songs in the thick air.

The child, seen from the back like this, could be a boy or a girl. Marian can see only softly cupped-under brown hair against a chubby neck, and stubby little fingers parading a collection of tiny dolls and colored beads by, or, lacking those, marching by themselves, ten little make-believe somethings that only the child can appreciate. Whose child could it be?

Marian thinks of her own children; they will be getting home from school soon. To Grandma Irene. Bradley, so like Adam in his melancholy heart tucked behind clown's antics, Melanie, so unlike anyone they'd ever been able to think of— "a changeling" Adam assures her—and Stephen, the child of her heart. She has left them wandering the lobby and gift shop area many times during the last few months. She wonders now if they might have discovered this tiny chapel and sat humming, waiting, as this child is now.

Marian searches the facts and, finding no happy resolution, decides to stay here in this oasis of respite until there's a chance Adam has been, as they say, "installed." Then maybe she'll be able to face the grim, determined captives of the glassed-in cage that is the ICU waiting room. It reminds her of their aquarium at home, where the tiny colorful prisoners suck eagerly, futilely, at the sides and bottom, darting hopefully to the surface at any crumb of possibility. She'd rather wait here. Several "shoulds" shove in at her peace—should she call her mother, her friends? Should she go put Adam's things in the car?

Should she go on up to ICU now?—but weariness possesses her and shoves her down into inertia. She will wait.

The sudden, crushing weariness is like damp cold in her bones; it doesn't seem as if any amount of rest could ever alleviate it. Yet she is not sleepy and her wide eyes will not close against the facts of the day. She can only slump and slide her eyes back and forth over the room, over the realities, like a vigilant lizard. The lighting, meant to spotlight the altar area, makes a smoky shaft filled with tiny lively forms like a microscope field. The child's head occasionally intersects it, making a halo. The child is a girl, Marian sees now, a tiny red satin ribbon fixing her hair and her gender. Someone has left their little girl here alone. Who? Whose little girl is she? Marian expands it into an object of concern, something to think about besides the bloody mess she's just witnessed.

The sweet humming stops and the little girl looks over her shoulder toward the door. The innocent longing on her face tells Marian she must be waiting for her mother, that the humming little parades no longer hold her attention. When she turns fully, spying Marian at the back, Marian can see plainly that hers is beyond a child's temporary innocence; she is a Down's Syndrome child, Mongoloid, as they used to say. There are the telltale genetic idiosyncrasies in her forehead, the gray eyes, guileless mouth, the busy tongue that does not want to stay in her mouth. The child smiles, wary at first but more broadly as she sees Marian's bland smile in return. But, as if remembering some admonition, she turns back to her play.

As Marian lets a few more long minutes slide by, the child holds up first one doll, then another, then the colored beads one by one; lifts them up into the smoky shaft of light, watching the dusty particles dance and swirl around them. Marian wonders if the child comprehends her own poignancy in some way; can she know she is a source of pity? Can Adam? Is she herself a source of pity to anyone, Someone? Dare she even speak the name of One who, observing from the dim recesses, might pity her even now? Would He look with pity on her idiot's face? If she could only hold the pieces innocently up to the light . . .

Suddenly she is running as if pursued. Down the hall, elevators, doors, more doors. Frantic. Could she have missed the "installation"? The ICU waiting area "aquarium" is full. Those waiting are obscured by plastic plants like noonday perch under a pier, darting out at the slightest stimulation. Sometimes doctors tap on the glass to signal a waiting relative to swim over. Marian quickly scans the faces inside; most scan her too, ever hopeful of catching sight of their doctor or a favorite nurse. Seeing no one familiar, she goes and taps lightly on the heavy ICU door, then pushes it slightly open to flag someone down.

"Mr. Stauffer?" she asks timidly, "Have they brought Mr. Stauffer up yet?"

"Are you his wife?"

"Yes."

"They just called from Radiology. They'll be bringing him up to room 'C' in a half hour or so."

"Do you know his condition?"

"Well, he's on a respirator I guess you know. But stable otherwise I think. He won't be my patient. Jenny will have him and she's in with another patient right now. If you'd care to wait out in the waiting room we'll call you when we have him stabilized and cleaned up. You can see him for a few minutes then. Outside of that, well, the visiting hours are on the door."

Marian knows the hours only too well. Remembers Jenny

too from before, even though this attendant is new. She breathes now; Adam is alive.

It is Dr. Yee who finally comes with crumbs of hope to the glass tank. In his litany of events, made precise and staccato by his foreign accent, Marian notices that the "fifty-cent words," as Bradley calls them, are all really only modest euphemisms: exudates, petechiae, urinary, flatulence. They allow them both to be modest and reasonable about the filthy business before them.

"We've put him completely asleep, Mrs. Stauffer, and knocked his own respiratory responses out with Pavlon so he won't fight the respirator. You can go in and see him a moment, but he won't know you're there. He'll be comatose at least until tomorrow. We want to get his blood gases stabilized, so we can't have him fighting the respirator."

Marian pictures Adam as Pecos Bill, smashing the respirator with a mighty fist. But when the doctor guides her into the cubicle they call room C she is overcome. Impossible that this strutted nude is Adam. No neat TV hospital soap opera this. A dry, cracked "oh my God" escapes her parched lips. He looks like a toppled mannequin in a Radio Shack window display; the maze of hardware around him is overwhelming enough in itself, but the actual physical person is beyond anything she can imagine or accommodate. All props are gone— glasses, watch, clothes, underwear, slippers. He is nude, with only a light sheet thrown halfheartedly across his genitals. Even that reveals its own tangle of tubing and tape.

He seems a startled crucifix, with arms flexed, palms upward, revealing angry red stigmata. His eyes, partly open, give the startled look. But it is only the narcotic tension, the nurse explains. Tape, tubing, and electrical wires crisscross his bare chest—Gulliver defeated by malevolent Lilliputians.

But the worst is the airway crammed down his throat, tongue forced cruelly to one side. It gags Marian to even look. There is no question of escape. He is trussed up as thoroughly as a turkey, the cruel tube tied and taped into splitting lips in case the swollen tongue should awaken and attempt escape. Even his poor suppliant hands are tied to the bed rails. No, no question of escape. It would take Houdini, an act of God, and a cast of thousands to free him.

"He will be like this at least until his blood gases improve, maybe sometime tomorrow, Mrs. Stauffer. You can go home and get some rest. If you just leave your number with the nurses they will call you if there is any change."

She watches Adam for another long moment, the mechanically rhythmic breathing. Only the electronic hills feeding out on the eerie green scope assure her that he is alive. That and the vague assumption that more violence would ensue should he give up the struggle. She thinks she might faint; a wave of nausea washes over her. She knows she can't stay, must get out of here.

Running, blinded, she is almost out the front door before she remembers the sack in the chapel. Hurrying back in she grabs it and spins around, her face already losing its public composure. A great, choking dry sob escapes before she can stop it and she sinks to the pew, hugging the lumpy grocery sack to her. She finds her grief oddly dry, however, somehow beyond tears.

After she has cried this curious dry gasping for what seems hours, she realizes someone is watching her. The child is gone from the front pew; no one was here when she came in. But a complete turn reveals a man in the dim foyer, leaning against the "Guest Registry" table. She at first takes him for a youth, lounging against the table in careless ease. But a clerical collar gives him away. She gathers her parcels as if to rise, but he walks over and intercepts her.

"I don't mean to intrude on your privacy, ma'am," he offers hurriedly. "My name's Michael Slovacek. I'm the acting chaplain here at the hospital this week; were you perhaps looking for me?"

He is earnest; she is terrified. There is nothing intimidating in his appearance or demeanor: short, his head too big in proportion to his body; fifties, maybe, grizzled face and graying hair that won't quite behave. But she doesn't want to talk to anyone. But the long, bony hand he offers is warm, sincere; she relents.

"No. I mean, I've been coming here to think. It's all right isn't it? Am I in the way or anything?"

This makes him laugh. "No, I'm afraid it's me who's in the way here. I've been out of the office and just thought maybe you'd been waiting to talk to the chaplain or something. Since you've inadvertently got me anyhow perhaps I could offer you some coffee and Kleenex. Free! A public service, you know . . ." as he talks, laughing softly to himself as if at a pleasant tale, he steers her gently to the open office off the foyer. She cannot resist the insistent pressure and finds herself in a small office, cluttered with magazines, books, and paperwork and smelling of freshly brewed coffee. He leaves the door open to the dim foyer as if he might be waiting for someone to come by.

He hands her a box of tissues and a hot mug of coffee which she leans over, breathing the warm, fragrant steam, letting the moisture collect a moment around her mouth and nose.

"Troubles here at the hospital?"

"It's my husband. He's in ICU."

He nods knowingly, busying himself around the room as he talks. "Tough, huh?"

"The pits." She thinks of Adam's peach pits in Mexico and almost smiles.

"Heart?"

"No. Cancer."

"Yeah," he sighs, and nods as if in agreement with a longer account of facts. He pops the collar off as if escaping a cardboard manacle.

"It's not really mine," he says noting her interest in the collar. "I'm just covering for a friend here and have found his collar to be a more efficient hall pass than my explanations. Makes me look more priestly, I suppose. You Catholic?"

"No."

"So you won't mind my not being too ecclesiastical?" His voice tilts up a second, but he doesn't seem to expect an answer.

"My friend, the real chaplain around here, wears the cardboard noose. Says he'd wear a monk's robe if they'd let him. Something about visually preparing people to receive . . ."

She is comforted by the warmth of the coffee, the ease of this man's manner, the fact that he busies himself elsewhere and she can respond or not as she chooses. The room itself is comforting, a tiny utilitarian space of desk, chairs, window, bookshelves, and coffeepot. The debris is only superficial, maybe even only a week's worth of this man's—did he say his name was Michael?—unrelated clutter.

"What did you say your name was?"

"Michael. Just Michael, please. There's 'Slovacek' too but it's such an auditory name and leaves the problem of how to spell it. Just Michael."

He reminds Marian of a TV detective, pacing, nursing a pencil tip instead of a cigar, chopping off his ramblings, one eye squinted against half-truths. And knowing more than he's telling.

"Adam, my husband, has had cancer several months now, but doing pretty well all in all. The treatment has been very intensive; neither of us has been able to continue working. It's like we were just sucked out of the real world and into this one and have never really had time to look back. We're insulated here; stuck on this really weird island and we can't get back. This today, well, I really don't know. A 'respiratory arrest' they called it. They had to put him on a respirator. Adam made me promise never to let them hook him up to life support equipment . . . but, well, when they tell you he'll die without it, everything's different." Marian is surprised by her own torrent of words, her eagerness to tell this perfect stranger her burdens.

"Of course it is. You have to let them do anything that might help, don't you?" His unruly hair bobs up and down with his head; his eyes are sweet and soft beneath his grizzled, pock-marked face. He is settling down across the desk from her now with his own steaming cup of pungent coffee.

"Have you been into ICU? Seen what they do to them? They have him trussed up like a Christmas turkey . . ." Tears spring to her eyes again.

"Like they've strangled the very life out of him with some bizarre mechanical apparatus and are forcing it back," Michael commiserates, not even surprised.

"Exactly." Marian falls back in the chair, relieved to entrust the mental picture to his words.

"I myself have wondered a thousand times if we haven't

grabbed something central out of God's hands. We hear people say all the time how critically ill people are in the hands of God, yet when we see such elaborate efforts to hold onto them . . . A sort of electronic no-man's-land of the human soul."

"Adam's been through so much. And now . . . maybe I've just made the easy choice for myself, or just made the worst choice for the kindest reasons. You should see him . . ."

They are interrupted by a phone call and with an apologetic shrug Michael picks the phone up and paces with it, keeping up his end of an enigmatic conversation. Marian had almost forgotten that he is a minister until now, hearing the soothing responses peppered with "God's will" and "bathed in prayer." The words that smell of religion bring to mind the needlework homilies and garish bumper stickers she hates. Like the first road sign approaching Smithville that had said that "Jesus is the answer" long before the Seniors of '65 had asked "What was the question?" As she watches, safe behind her warm wall of coffee vapor, he picks up a large Bible and settles across the desk with it. Its soft brown cover is cracked and worn, the edges of gilt all but gone, turned up into a swollen bloom so that they are thicker than the body. Marian is transfixed as he reads to the invisible party on the telephone. Then he abruptly hangs up.

"Sorry for the interruption."

"No, no. Perfectly all right. I'm afraid it was me who interrupted you. You've been so kind I'd almost forgotten you are a minister."

He laughs and she realizes what she has said. She cannot help laughing too.

"Not to worry," he says, reading her stricken face. "Grace doesn't preclude the possibility of pain, you know. It is there

before, during, and after the pain, larger than the sorrow."
His eyes are sad, though, even as he speaks to her of joy. She
knows he would say more if she would ask.

"It would be unfair of me to talk 'grace' with you; I have
to tell you that I've never gotten anything out of religion. And
I've tried! I really think I have. I'm not a believer; at least I
have my own beliefs."

"Most of the people who come in here are mad at God,
Marian." He stops and flings his hands up: "And RABID
about preachers!" His smile is disarming. "But He doesn't
mind, I'm sure of it. God's a lot humbler than most folks
think."

He is not afraid of the silence that falls on them and they
let it lie between them like the steam from the fresh coffee.

"Were you raised in a church?"

"Oh, yes. My mother 'did right' by me."

"And?"

"I . . . we have looked and only found fluff in the church.
When Adam began to fail physically he started asking a lot
of spiritual questions; well, we both did. All I found in my
childhood church was TA and motorcycle Zen. He even tried
some of the TV evangelists; they were the worst. Hucksters,
Adam calls them."

His laughter is a relief; she is afraid she is being rude, af-
fronting him, somehow, to so malign his trade. "Don't apologize to me, I know exactly what you mean." He pulls out a
pipe, but never fills or lights it. "We're rhinestone cowboys,
some of us."

"But how can anyone know what's true, there are so many
interpretations . . . How do even you ever choose?"

"The truth is all right there," he lays one hand on the bulky

97

brown Bible, "but nobody wants it. Just won't have it. No big theological or historical or archaeological objection either," he emphasizes, sensing her next objections before she voices them, "but something soft and jaded . . . too much TV maybe. Artists used to be crazy for the truth, wanted to replicate it precisely. Until cameras came along. When actual truth came along the artists dropped that and went to personal expression or impression. The cat was out of the bag: what they'd wanted all along was never truth, but an expression of self. Even with Truth available here," patting the worn book, "in genuine cowhide, they won't have it." He shakes his head in genuine regret, but turns back to her, brightening, "Well, 'Truth forever on the scaffold, lies forever on the throne' I think it goes. Lowell, wasn't it?"

"I don't know. Adam would."

"A book person, eh?"

"Words, books, yes. He's even keeping a journal of his illness. Adam reads the classified ads for relaxation." There is a long silence as Marian finishes her coffee. "Thank you so much for your kindness, but I think I'd better be getting home; the kids will be wondering."

He holds one hand out, palm up. "What do you think; shall we pray for your Adam?"

"I hope you will, reverend. I'd rather not; well, it's a long story."

"That ends with 'He might not answer'?"

"Well, yes," surprised, disarmed.

"And you say you're not a believer! There's a corner reserved for Him somewhere, to be so concerned about His reputation."

The window behind Michael is darkening as night falls, and

she can see her own pale face reflected there. "I'll think about what you've said; just can't absorb it right now . . ."

"Oh, of course," he looks genuinely alarmed. "I'm not challenging you, Mrs. Stauffer, just sharing my own thoughts. I'd like to help, but I know there's precious little anyone can do at a time like this. But please know I'm available here if you'd like to stop by again. You'll have a lot on your mind, I know."

"I want to understand though; I just wish I could let everything in at once. Just know."

"Yes, myself . . . But it's like entering a dark room. Your eyes eventually adjust to let in whatever light there is, but never all at once. It's the order of things."

He is so sure of this last, and so comfortable in his acceptance of her doubts that she has to smile again. She can scarcely imagine what he sees around here most days, how narrow must be his own beliefs. Yet he warmed her in the middle of her cold tragedy. She can move, and breathe again. She considers asking him to go with her to look at Adam, Gulliver snared and wounded, one last time, say good night. But the doctor had assured her there would be no response at least until tomorrow. She doubts they would let her in at this off-hour anyway. Rising to leave, she only takes his outstretched hand and thanks him.

"You're so welcome. Please stop by any time. I'm going to slip up and check on your husband tonight before I leave. Just remember: 'This too shall pass.' "

"Adam always says that."

"From Job."

"He swears it's from Jerry Lewis."

9

This is the longest dream yet; Adam plows doggedly through
the details he can understand. There must be meaning embedded somewhere in this rubble, if he can only follow each
separate thought. It does no good to open his eyes; the only
part of the mechanical debris he can understand is the huge
black and white clock. But the hour means nothing to him.
There is no day or night in this place; every moment is a blaze
of lights and mechanical noises. Not even a window so that
he can get his bearings. If there were only a window, a point
to tell him day from night, east from west. Or is that blaze the
window over the kitchen sink at home? It is all too confusing;
he can't fight it. The instant the voices and hands go away, he
slips back into the dreams.

He is a child again; hears his mother calling him, "Adam,
Adam," so soft, so sure.

"Here, Mother," he answers, and when she turns to him
she is taller than anyone. The shadows fall like veils around

her, the evening lights twinkle like stars in her hair. Then they fall around him, envelop him and swoop him up to where he is taller than anyone too. Hello, hello, all the voices say to him. Mr. Stauffer, Mr. Stauffer. Adam, can you hear me? Yes, yes, of course. What do you want? But they never answer, maybe they can't hear him, though he speaks clearly, loudly. "Eee-nun-cee-ate cleeeer-ly," Mrs. Pope, high school English, always said. He can feel his lips articulate each syllable, enunciating to make Mrs. Pope proud, then Marian putting some kind of ointment on them. With the soothing moisture he realizes how dry and cracked they are. Or no . . . He is so small, it must be his mother.

"Here, Adam, this is for you." His mother puts something in his hand—a small tin of waxy pomade, round and the size of a silver dollar. The top falls when he lifts the gummy fingerful to his chapped lips. "Keep it in your pocket," she says, swooping down to reconnect the lid and bottom. His very own to put on whenever he wants; Fina and his mother won't chase him down and smear it on him. He uses it again almost before it warms in his pocket, practicing, marveling to be so big, until he is ready to take it out so slow, so careful in front of Blake.

Riding across the split, patched seat from Blake in the old pickup, he twirls and twirls the tin in his pocket. Then eases it out and opens it, laying the riskier top precisely next to the more stable bottom in the palm of his hand. Then a tiny dab for the still-coated lips. But before he can complete the performance a bump tosses both to the floor, ointment side down. Before he can rescue them, Blake has gathered them and tossed them to the cluttered dash. "I'll keep it for you if you can't keep from droppin' it."

．   ．   ．

Many voices coax him. Turn over, lie back, settle down, wake up. They can't make up their minds. And they still can't seem to hear him. One prays, not exactly the formal sonorous blessing of Blake over meals and Bible reading, but neither the fervent prayers his mother used to whisper into his feverish neck. No, this sounds like a simple friend. A friend of God.

His own hands are folded, acquiescent. He could float into nothingness again, but there is a stirring, like rustling leaves. Like a mighty rushing wind, shaken. Oh, God, I never said no to You; haven't been speaking to You, actually, lo these many years, Hound of Heaven, Sir. Soft, distant laughter; the man who prays is smiling at him. Who is he? Perhaps they know each other. But he cannot respond, can only float in this heavy air. Or is it water? No . . . thicker than water. Blood is thicker than water.

Days of vigilance and ingratiating behavior pay off; by the end of the week Adam is an old-timer in ICU and Marian can slip in to visit him at odd times, as long as she doesn't attract attention or stay too long. Once by his bedside she often only stands and stares, terrified of the mechanical clutter. She notices the nurses applying glycerin to Adam's cracked lips and begins to do so herself when she is there. Adam looks at her sometimes as if he knows her, but she can't be sure. He wakes enough to fight the respirator and trigger its alarm system, summoning flocks of attendants. A never-ending tension between life and death. "Choose life," she whispers to Adam, over and over.

The shock never lessens and the little chapel downstairs has become a welcome refuge. Today Adam's restlessness seems to be contagious. Marian walks down to spend some quiet time, maybe visit with Michael a moment. When she enters, the little Down's Syndrome girl greets her with an expansive wave, recognizing her after so many visits. Marian remembers a tiny pen and notebook set in her jacket pocket, a gift shop memento she had planned to take home to Melanie. On impulse, she extends it to the girl. "Here, I brought you a present. What is your name?"

"Debbie." Debbie. Easy. That much she is sure of.

"Well, Debbie, I am Marian." She repeats it to see if Debbie will say it. But no, she is already busy with a tiny picture on one of the bright pages. Just like Melanie would have been.

Marian slips into the pew farthest from the door and sinks down into the welcome dim silence. There is an ever-escalating mountain of facts she has to sort through. A lot of knowledge and no wisdom. Before she can ever get attached to one version another comes. One doctor after another with the ever-changing "truth" about things. Michael had talked to her about "higher truth" yesterday. This is the slippery truth about truth, as far as she can tell: that it changes all the time. The first sorrow of life is unleashed in childhood; the others only scratch at the valiant scab of that first wound. A wound we seem to like being reminded of, endlessly and mindlessly rubbing it to elicit that familiar ache. Oh yes, we say to it, over and over. I know you. But the familiarity never breeds contempt.

"Adam likes to pray with me," Michael tells her one day. "He can't talk, of course, but he folds his hands and prays as sweet as a little boy."

"He does?" She is embarrassed. And glad. "Well, his parents raised him in the church." It seems a bumbling excuse, somehow. Like she didn't have her homework because the dog ate it; Adam prayed because his parents raised him in the church. Yet she likes the thought that Michael saw him like a little boy; she thinks of him that way herself so often.

"Was he a believer?"

"Adam? Does Adam believe in God?" Not such a complicated question that she should stutter so.

"Yes."

"He says he does, yes. He says it's people he's not sure about."

What can God be thinking, anyway, Marian wonders more and more. He is only a distant reality, like her father. Her father was charming in a way, she supposes—her mother had obviously fallen for him once—but heartless. What was God thinking during those first long, dark sorrows of childhood; where was He then? And now, lost in a maze—no Plan, this. Are the Alpha and the Omega all we get? Do we have to muddle through the middle ourselves? Where can You be; what can You be thinking?

The chapel this evening is too warm; the whole hospital seems like it needs to throw the doors and windows open and breathe. The air is just too stale and overworked. Marian feels her face becoming hot.

"God has promised that He won't give us more than we can bear," Michael begins.

"Who gets to decide when that is?" Marian breaks in. "I mean, I can take a lot when it's my own needle digging for a splinter or peeling a scab. But when I'm at someone else's mercy the pain is always more than I can bear." She's heard the empty words before, from people she didn't like so much.

Michael's eyes are sad as they rock back and forth, casting about his mind for an answer. "I am inadequate, Marian, to answer the question you are really asking. Why *is* there so much suffering in the world? Why *do* these things happen to good people? Anything I could say to justify suffering would only make you hate me. I can only tell you, with all tenderness, that God loves us with an almost pathetic longing." He rises and takes Marian's coffee cup and refills it from the steaming pot. "He is the Father who put his own ring on the returning prodigal son, without a whisper of 'I told you so.' That son suffered fear and pain and loneliness and shame—all our sufferings—but his father was there to meet him with grace and great joy. He will be there to meet you and Adam."

"If I have faith . . ." Marian mars the hypnotic beauty of his words with her own doubt.

"Just think of faith as a bridge that forms under your feet as you step out on it."

They are both silent for a long while, the distant hospital traffic the only sound. Marian thinks how much she wishes Michael's words were true, relaxes under the tenderness with which he says them. But when she goes over her experience in her mind, fishing for something to add credence to what he says, only old wounds and disappointments will surface.

"Church people think everything is so simple. Or act as if it is, until the rules start. I would rather be free, even falling free, than trapped by some cosmic set of rules I cannot understand." The air hangs still and heavy between them. "And I won't have a lie, or even any wishful thinking."

"No, I can see that you won't."

"If religion helps people, they should go for it."

"But it doesn't . . ."

"If *faith* helps them, they should have faith. In whatever helps them."

"No . . ."

"I myself just want someONE to help me. Get me out of this mess. Get Adam and me out. I don't want a cab ride to take me where I want to go, or a crutch. Cars break down. Religion breaks down. I want real help. Help that won't break down."

"Of course you do."

"I even tried drugs once. To help. They worked too, altered my perceptions just enough to where I could manage. But, of course, that broke down too." Her fear that she might cry evaporated under a clear, dry-eyed, staring exhaustion.

"Yes." Michael sat stock-still, as if listening for a faint cue, or lost in reverie.

"I cannot believe. Can you understand that, Michael? I want to, understand. Even feel that I should be able to. But I can't. What can be done about that? How can anybody make themselves believe what they simply don't believe? I was raised to go through the motions and I don't want that. I want to pull the whole tree up and plant it somewhere else."

"I know exactly what you mean. Even so, Marian, some dirt always clings to the roots . . ."

"I'm just so scared . . ." She stops and gathers up her things slowly, thinking. Then meets his steady gaze: "But you've been so kind. I surely don't want you to think that it's you I'm rejecting."

"Nor quite God, I have a feeling, Marian."

The night has worn long in the ICU waiting area, but Marian is determined to catch the doctors. It's ten days now and Adam doesn't seem any better or worse. The crowd has thinned out, down to the handful of grim, determined waiting friends and relatives. Some have been at it so many nights that they have a routine just as if they were home: blankets from the nurses' station, juice and chips from the vending machines, ten-minute ritual in the public restroom. Just no dogs or cats to put out one last time. No more doctors come to tap on the glass, offering hope to the frightened fish within.

Marian is beginning to look more kindly toward them herself, sympathy for their worn, harried expressions, she is sure. Or the Stockholm effect. Will they give her more than she can bear? Some are kinder than others, as are the nurses that care for Adam. Some will accommodate her at odd hours, work with her on little points of Adam's comfort. But none of their expressions would she call mercy. What would mercy be? A cure? Relief? An end? How much kindness would it take to become mercy? Or is it a different thing altogether? Where is this grace Michael is so sure of?

By the next morning's ten minutes allotted visiting time, she is calmer at Adam's bedside. Love and anger come clear in alternating patterns, like a faulty tuner knob, receiving conflicting signals. Even the pity, to see him like this, will not keep the anger away. Or maybe it is just the exhaustion.

"Adam?" She whispers his name softly, just enough to let him know she's there if he's only resting, not enough to wake him if he's actually asleep.

Adam's blue eyes fly open. They are not so red now, and the lashes are damp. She can tell that he sees her clearly. Marian is surprised. He turns his face slightly to her, with some effort due to the awkward tubing. But that slight degree of turn allows a spill of tears and Marian reflexively reaches out to wipe them before they can trickle into . . . what? What could she be saving from those tears? Her own eyes fill and then spill also as she leans over to kiss the two square inches of his hot forehead that this disaster has left them.

Adam's own hands are still tied, but Marian can tell that he is conscious enough now to be trusted with them free. She calls a nurse in and they untie his hands and explain as he asks a dozen silent questions with them, pointing and gesturing around the room, himself, and the blinking, hissing monster that breathes for him. Marian starts at the irregular jarring and hissing that finally sets off the respirator's alarm. The nurse encourages Adam to relax and let the machine have its way.

"Now that you're waking up, Mr. Stauffer, the doctors will begin to turn down the machine's sensitivity, start letting you trigger it. Finally of course, you'll be breathing without it and we can take it out," the nurse drones on as she adjusts dials and writes down numbers on his chart.

At this hope, Adam's eyes brighten and he nods and looks to Marian. The poignant eagerness of a child. They are children; Hansel and Gretel lost in the forest for so long, but healing each other's losses. Holding hands, loving each other, making it all be all right, right up until the oven. But the witch is tricked for now; they are free from the flames.

"Yes, Adam. Yes." Marian cannot say more, but only holds his hand and wipes his eyes with a tissue.

With his hands free, Adam can tell them to take the cover down and turn on the fan and wipe his face. All the dormant little urges that mean life. He gradually seems satisfied, almost comfortable. Late in the long day, he is able to write Marian a shaky note: "Am I hot?" And those damp blue eyes smile their secret joke at Marian.

Tears and laughter sprint into her throat at once and she chokes a moment with the struggle. Recovering, she touches a finger to her own tongue and then to Adam's face, making a sizzling sound. And kisses him once again on his damp forehead.

10

After three and a half weeks camping out in the ICU waiting area and another two weeks with Adam back in a regular room, Marian feels like some pitiful phantom lurking in the bowels of the hospital. She knows when the fresh coffee is brewed in the nurses' work station and which nurses won't mind if she has some. And she learns quickly how to get things done: who to ask next when one nurse doesn't bring Adam's pain medication in time, which aide will get fresh linens quickly when needed, which supervisors will act on her complaints. She can spot each of Adam's doctors in a crowd of fifty white coats, recognizes their voices as they exit the elevator clear down on the other end of the long hall. And she can tell what food will be served in the cafeteria once she sees what they bring on Adam's tray.

Today they've brought Salisbury steak, mashed potatoes, and the ubiquitous Jello. The diet card says "Soft," but they haven't figured out just how soft it would have to be for Adam to get it down. Pureed and diluted by half would be more like it.

"Adam, wake up. Your lunch is here."

His eyes open so quickly and clearly that she knows he can't have really been asleep. He places one trembly finger over his tracheotomy tube at his throat and asks an airy "So soon? What time is it?" He points to his wrist, too, in case she doesn't understand the whispered sighs that are his voice now. He is weaned, as they put it, from the respirator, but the tube is still in place for security. Marian is glad the gelatin is green today, because Adam coughs up the leaked remains around the trach tube for an hour each time he eats. When it's red gelatin it looks like blood on his pajama front.

"Richard's going to help you with your lunch and then get you cleaned up. I'm going down to eat my lunch, then I'll be right back up. Okay?" She wonders if her "read-my-lips" messages are offensive to him. Has he lost his subtlety of understanding along with his subtlety of speech? She can't tell; anyway, they're more a verification to the aide that loiters with the tray. She has an agreement with him about lunch-time. The aide nods her out as he puts the tray down and greets Adam. Even though Adam is now long past caring about her helping him, she cannot tolerate the choking mess of meal-times and the heavy suctioning of Adam's trach tube that is necessary afterward. She has found it is better for them all if she just leaves for this half hour.

He coughs and gets the panicky look on his face that always comes with the coughing. Marian gets the oxygen tubing down from the valve on the wall; the doctors say to leave it off unless he needs it. "Are you getting enough air?" She holds the tubing poised and ready.

He holds his hand up to refuse the oxygen, then lies back and draws a slow, good breath. "An affair?"

"Enough air," she starts to repeat in her read-my-lips voice, then realizes he is teasing.

"Oh, Adam."

"Well, there's lots of young nurses here, you know. Richard here brings 'em in after you're gone." He only grins, not wanting to start up the coughing again with a real chest laugh. Richard chuckles and waves Marian away.

"I'm outta here, guys. No funny stuff 'til I get back."

"What we need here, Richard," she can hear him complaining as she steps into the hallway, "is prunes, not green gelatin. Prometheus bringing fire to earth was nothing compared to prunes . . ."

Something about the clogged hallways and myriad cubicles reminds Marian of the caves they used to dig endlessly when they were children. She can't remember how it ever started, whose idea it had been, but she knows they must have eventually covered most of the nearby vacant lots with their tunneling and caves and lean-to clubhouses. The bigger boys did most of the digging, while she and the others hustled scraps of plywood, posts, wire, whatever they could scavenge from neighboring alleys. They laid the boards and scraps over the shallow rooms and connecting passageways, threw a thin layer of dirt on top, and crawled into their own world.

Once she made her own cave near home and ran about twelve extension cords together so it could boast a naked, hanging bulb. Her last happy memory of childhood was of sitting down in that damp, dim hole, reading and playing the radio. The books had finally curled with the damp, the layers of paper and cellophane separating into a yellowed bloom whose pages would barely turn. She had planned to be a botanist then, in that straightforward time before the world tilted and she fell off into a bitter adolescence and "real life."

"Mrs. Stauffer! Marian . . ." Michael Slovacek's warm voice is familiar now, too.

"Hello." She turns and extends her hand, genuinely glad to see him.

"How are you today? And Adam?"

"Good, Michael. The doctors don't give much hope, of course, for the long run. But Adam's stable and the tracheotomy is healing well, they say."

"That's wonderful," Michael says, beaming.

"And," Marian interrupts, smiling. "You won't believe this part. They say he can be discharged in a few days."

"You're kidding!" His surprise and delight match her own.

"Nope. The doctors all agree there's nothing more to try in the way of treatments for the cancer. Just try to let him rest and recover from this bout. Go home to live out his days."

"Well, you never know . . ." Michael says softly.

"No, that's for sure. And speaking of surprises, we'll be going to Texas, to Adam's father's farm, when the kids get out of school for Christmas vacation. Adam wants to and it might be good for all of us." She shifts her purse and looks back to Adam's room. "Look, I'm just going down for a quick lunch. Would you care to join me? My treat."

"Oh, I wish I could, but I have to meet my daughter for lunch. A rain check?"

"Sure, anytime you say."

"I've just time to see Adam a few minutes. Is this a good time?"

"Yes, actually, it is. It only takes him a few minutes to cough up what 'liquid diet' he can choke down. Henderson's with him. Let Adam tell you about home and all. The Valley. Then you can see what you think."

"Great. I have something I want him to read." He holds up a thin volume with tabs of paper markers sticking out.

"He'll be glad. He's still working on the little book you gave him the other day. He's been too sick to concentrate, but seems to be coming around now, making more of an effort. I know he'll feel more normal when he's back to clipping articles and writing in his journal."

"He really loves books, doesn't he?"

"He says he likes to suspend his disbelief. But I'm sure it's a literary notion, not a theological one!"

"Right." His eyes shine.

"And don't be asking him any of those generic questions. He's shooed away two Baptists and a Catholic today."

"Thanks for the warning. I'll be careful. And original, if at all possible," he says, with his easy grin.

Marian is surprised how easily she walks this thin, cordial line of sanity now while all the bombs of illness and loss fall around her. Michael Slovacek's warmth and kindness, if not his faith, give her comfort. Her ability to believe in anything beyond that must have been stunted in childhood. So many things you thought were true, thought you could count on, disappointed. The desire for facts slithered through wastelands of opinions, shifting with the wind. Even the animals she'd been so sure went on the ark two by two. Come to find out there were seven of some of them.

Adam's young resident, Dr. Perry, pointed out that even medicine was forever changing its mind: the cure for diverticulosis in the old Merck Manual that Adam had was a low-residue, low-roughage, low-bulk diet. Dr. Perry's new Merck proclaimed it (arrogant, certain, disdainful) to be a high-bulk, high-fiber one.

Michael had agreed with so many of her own objections, she wondered how he'd kept his own faith. "They're selling Him like toothpaste," she'd ventured.

"Yes," he'd agreed, his bushy head bobbing in slow regret.

"It's just a bunch of rules to most people."

"Yes, sadly, that's true. I think that must have been Adam and Eve's problem; and people still say, 'We don't want a relationship with you, God . . . just give us the rules and don't bother us.' "

Sometimes his words come back, humming in her mind, like an old familiar tune. One she might remember if she could just hear a few more strains: Anger does not displace love, it proves it. We do not hate what we have never loved. Do not take into account a wrong suffered. (But you'll excuse me if I don't come back for more.) Love is the most powerful force in the universe. (Then what is the second most powerful force?) Anyway, what could anyone say that could even touch the misery around her every day now?

She cannot resist stepping into the chapel a moment on her way to the cafeteria. Only her little friend is there, as usual, humming to herself on the front pew. There are new entries in the guest registry, and Marian feels as if she personally has missed visitors. Brave little blossoms of hope, these scribblings, in the face of disaster. She wishes she could gather them, pick them off the page, hold them to her. She herself has none to offer. "No hope," the doctors say now. No hope. But we will press on, with hope or without it. That next step may take them to a hidden cavern where this disease cannot touch

them. Where it maybe never even happened at all. Angels, beautiful and good, will guard them while they heal.

She loves the dim peace here in the chapel, a respite from the brightness and animation of Adam's room. Is it fear that makes the nurses too loud, the doctors too quick, everyone too animated? Even at home it rattled, that fear in its mail armor. Even Blake, terse usually to the point of rudeness, had become nearly garrulous.

"I always wanted Adam to have it better than I did," he had offered, "but to have it the same way."

Hearing the regret, Marian had not answered.

"Part of me wanted him to have things; part of me thought he should struggle for them too. Like I did; and my own father."

"Adam knows that," she had answered carefully. She had thought herself, many times, that even the best parent has to turn on their own child at some point, for both their sakes. It had surely been Blake's love that made him so hard on Adam. She can easily forgive him that, but cannot stoop to recover the lost tie with her own mother, guilty only of the same sins.

And this child before her now, little Debbie, whose tiny chromosomal difference assures her only a brief and lonely hold on life—what can she know about the sins of her fathers? What kind of love can leave her sitting here alone nearly every day? Yet she hums to herself happily enough, and fills the little chapel with her sweet innocence.

There are just too many things beyond understanding. They are getting frantic over the hospital bill, already cresting the hill of a hundred thousand dollars. Yet just a while back someone paid nearly forty million dollars for an oil painting of some wilting sunflowers. Would the mad, one-eared Van

Gogh have laughed or cried if he had known? She had asked Adam what he thought Van Gogh would have done with all that money.

"Started a television ministry."

And the art she had been so immersed in at work seems so distant now, like choosing wallpaper. Her first love had been the ancient attempts at art by primitive man. Spears and stones engraved with female figures or geometric designs or painted with red ochre, some dated at 25,000 to 30,000 B.C. It had thrilled her to think that so long ago, in his dank, smoky cave, someone had felt the urge toward beauty, needed to create in addition to survive. Robust mammoth-hunter or childless woman or crippled youth left behind alone? Now, in the face of this daily gore and Adam's slow demise, "art" seems like remote craft, has no bearing on daily life. Or what is her daily life now in this white tile cave.

What should she do? She really doesn't want to go to the Valley, but Adam is insistent and they do need the help. What can she do? Who can she even ask? Her mother and Blake have helped as much as they could, but neither one can help much with the overwhelming bills. The administration at Alpha has stretched Adam's benefits beyond her expectations, but the salary will end soon. They will have some money from the pension account, and the CD that they've saved for Stephen's college. But after that? She tries not to speculate, is learning her way around the frustrating maze of filing insurance forms and juggling payments. Robbing Peter to pay Paul, Adam calls it, though he seems to have all but lost interest in how she accomplishes it. Adam's benefits at Alpha proved to be wonderful health insurance and wonderful life insurance, but no disability or income protection other than the retirement fund.

Blake has advised her to take that out as cash and use it; whatever is left can be invested later. Later. Well, she won't think about that either.

The kids are exhausted and confused by the erratic schedules, by plans that are always tentative. They sometimes wander as listlessly as Adam's dogs around and around the house, looking for some order, some cheerful cohesiveness. It's hard to tell the role someone plays in your life until they are absent. Blake has offered to have them all stay at his South Texas farm when Adam is able to be discharged. Her mother has offered to come and live with them. Jessie can stay for short spells to relieve Marian. Adam will need so much care when he is discharged; she will be afraid to be at home alone with him. But how to stitch it all together into an everyday quilt they can still call life?

Her sigh echoes back to her in the nearly empty chapel as she forces herself to her feet and back out into the hallway where she literally runs into Michael.

"You okay, Marian?" He touches her arm lightly and Marian realizes she is crying.

"Yes. No. That is, well, I thought I was." She touches the tears on her face.

"News?"

"No, not really. I'm just trying to handle the news I already had. No hope. I guess I knew he couldn't be cured; I guess we knew that already."

"Well, there's always hope . . ."

"No, Michael, there isn't. Sometimes there is just more suffering. And no hope." The anger surprises her even more than the tears. "What happens when you just can't take any more?"

"God will not give you more than you can bear . . ."

"He already has, Michael. That's what I'm trying
you. But what do you know about suffering?" She knows
it is only the rage of nervous exhaustion. But she cannot stop
"You think you know so much about it all; how would you
know? Just because you hear the endless list of sorrows; that
doesn't make you an expert, does it? Maybe there's things
some of us on the receiving end know that you saints just
can't." She cringes to hear her own voice, venting all the pent-
up anger and frustration and fear.

"My Debbie and I know something about these things," he
offers quietly.

"Debbie?" blank, uncaring.

"Surely you know my Debbie? I thought you had even given
her a little gift awhile back . . ." Michael's face plainly shows
his surprise that she doesn't seem to put the facts together.

"Oh," is all she admits at first.

"My daughter."

"Oh, my God," and finally, "I'm so sorry, I really didn't
know." And quick tears of remorse.

"Oh, but no, no . . ." he is appalled at her discomfort. "I
say that only to share with you; I thought you already knew."

Spent, embarrassed, Marian follows him in to pick up his
little daughter for lunch. Amid Debbie's squeals of delight and
their old ritual of coffee and Kleenex, Michael fills in the details. How he and his wife had tried to have a baby for years;
and then, when all hope was gone, like a miracle, he'd said,
she was pregnant. How that miracle had taken her life and
left him with a severely handicapped child. Little Debbie, that
Marian has watched here for so long without realizing. So
that was why she was so often alone there; waiting, not for the

mother Marian had assumed, but for her father, the Reverend Michael Slovacek.

And still little Debbie's father has a passion for God. It is the first time she has seen behind Reverend Slovacek's office, seen that he is a man, a person, not an institution waiting there for her to embrace or scorn. He is Michael, a man who is drinking at the same bitter fountain that she finds herself drinking from even now . . .

"Well, time to go grab a bite to eat," she sighs.

"You could join us," Michael offers.

"No, thank you. I need a little time alone, I think."

As she rounds the corner of the tiny foyer, Marian lays a hand on the hard, cold, brass cross behind the registry. The high gloss leaves a smoky impression of her warm fingers for a moment when she lifts her hand again. Or had she only imagined it?

II

My lips are sayin' what they won't do:
Smoke, drink, lie to you.

Startin' tomorrow, I swear it's true,
I'll come home early, kiss only you.

These are the things I never will do:
Steal, cheat or lie to you.

Stephen hums the refrain to the country song with an audible "lie to you" between surges while Bradley pantomimes violent retching behind him just within Marian's view in the mirror. If Marian ignores the small oxygen tank and her recent memory, it's almost as if this long trip to South Texas is just another family vacation—Adam in the front seat, the kids wrestling in the back, the trunk full of their luggage. Adam has handled it pretty well, but anything more than five or so hours a day is too much for him, so it's been a long, slow trip.

Texas so far has lived up to its reputation for big: "The sun has ris, the sun has set, and here I is in Texas yet," Bradley chanted the old-time refrain. It wasn't until south of San Antonio that the world as Marian had known it began to fall away. Now, nearing the flat, dusty town of Alice, a couple of hours south of San Antonio, she thinks maybe they've all made a terrible mistake. It isn't just the trees and sloping hills she misses but the hallmarks of civilization like tall buildings and English advertisements—it's all official Tex-Mex from now on. It's another world, quaint in its own way, sort of a cross between the Mexican desert and a forties movie.

The addition of these wailing country-western songs of unrequited love is almost too much. Adam had turned Stephen's choice into a majority vote after "Who's Gonna Take Your Garbage Out When I'm Gone." Said his own interest was strictly sociological, as opposed to Stephen's, which was probably hormonal. The old sly grin had renewed her hope and won her vote. She had been so afraid he wouldn't tolerate the trip down, but he seems more himself than he has in weeks.

"I can't get around Farmer Fudd here." Marian's temper is short from trying to peer around the truck pulling a trailer with yet two more battered Port-a-cans being hauled to or from the fields.

"Yeah, I'm surprised the chamber of commerce didn't foresee the tourism problem."

"Longnecks and Port-a-cans," Bradley singsongs, "nowhere but Texas."

"And they say you can't go home again," Adam teases. His voice is still raspy and airy from the weeks on the respirator and the not-quite-healed tracheotomy. Marian wonders what it must feel like to have half your intended breath seep away before you can finish a sentence. She watches automatically now for the tremble and "off" skin color that means he isn't getting enough oxygen. The hilarity of the country songs seems to have lifted his spirits and improved his color for now. But she will be nervous until she has him checked in with the

Valley oncologist to whom Adam's records have been transferred, a Hispanic name she cannot remember or pronounce when she sees it. He has office hours twice a week in the small town of Teresita, only minutes from Blake's farm. They had talked to him by phone when their Chicago oncologist made the referral and he had assured them that the small hospital there in Teresita would be adequate. Anyway, there are larger medical centers in Harlingen and McAllen, only a half hour or so away. Pretty convenient by Chicago standards.

"Keep your shades on honey," Adam croons softly to her, "the motel's kinda crowded tonight."

"Adam, really . . ."

"But this is the top forty, Marian!"

"Yeah, Mom," Stephen adds from the back seat.

Marian and Bradley exchange helpless looks of despair in the mirror. Melanie is asleep in an impossible position, her slack mouth moving slightly in some quiet dream. Marian wonders, for the hundredth time this day, if it had been a good idea to come.

The first thought of it had come from Adam. Still weak and withdrawn since the respiratory crisis, he had put the case for going home to Texas surprisingly strong. "I need to go to the Valley and spend some time with Blake."

"But, why? He can come back soon and stay awhile. He's offered. Don't you think we'd better wait until you're stronger?" She persisted in the optimistic language they'd all adopted in spite of the consensus that Adam would probably never be any stronger.

"I have to go. You have to help me." His voice had been plaintive. "There's unfinished business . . . things I need to settle with Blake. Places I'd like to see again. Besides, there will be more help for you and distraction for the kids. And no snow to shovel."

"What about school? We can't just . . ."

"If we wait until the semester break it would be easy to transfer them down there for one semester."

She was dismayed that he meant something more than a brief visit. But he'd obviously been thinking it all out long enough to resolve the school issue in his mind. And Blake's farm, like some failed plantation hidden away in time, would solve many of their problems. They couldn't really afford the nurses that came for Adam's personal care. And every activity of the children had become a huge logistical problem because she couldn't leave Adam alone. He had only been home a few weeks, but already she was exhausting her resources and the friends she could ask to run errands or sit with Adam. Her own mother had gone home exhausted weeks ago. Blake's house-keeper, Fina, had practically raised Adam and could share the burden of his care; several of the farm hands helped with household things when necessary. It wasn't far to get around to places they needed to go, and Blake could help drive the kids and run errands. It had, indeed, always seemed strange: such a rugged little farm and comfortless house, but they were always spoiled by Fina and the others when they visited.

"And Fina could help you so we wouldn't need any more nurses," Adam had added, as if reading her thoughts. "Really, Marian, I want to. I know it's asking a lot of you. But it would just be for a few months. From Christmas until summer. Just one semester of school for the kids."

Without any transition he had gone on to explain his burial

wishes, hoping she would get plots for them both near his mother's grave. He had given it all to her in one bitter pill and then never mentioned it again. Home was important to Adam; he was always the first to tire of vacation trips, the most relieved to return after some crisis. Like some wounded animal he always wanted to drag his tired or hurt body back to familiar territory. Always going home, going home.

The stress of driving her entire family into this strange land is only a dull ache compared to the last six weeks. Adam's respiratory arrest and six-week hospital stay had burned away the dross, her visits with Michael keeping her afloat until that point at which she knew she would go under or go on. She had chosen then to cut away the variable of her feelings like ballast.

Clinging daily only to hope or habit, she learned—is learning still—to line up only the facts each day. The feelings were liars or imps; better she should make her plans without them. The dangers of introspection were too plain. She even began to see Adam's slow death as the proving ground for all the losses of life. It was at once bigger than just losing Adam and smaller. They had entered the long, uneven parade to the other side.

The words "He who loses his life shall gain it" come to her mind. Had Michael shared them with her? But she hadn't let their conversation run to "death," turning away like a shy lover. She was getting as superstitious as Fina, who thought a rooster crowing while facing the door of the house signified a coming death.

"You think Fina still has her chickens?" Marian wonders aloud.

"Well, a new generation of 'em, anyway," Adam nods.

"I'm not eating those orange eggs."

"Gross. Me neither. Liquid chicken," Bradley concurs and swoons, rolling his eyes back in his head.

"I like them," Stephen counters quietly.

"Yeah, well, you like Cindy Smalling, too, so we know what kind of taste you've got. Gross."

Bradley folds the map he has been worrying for the last hundred miles and pronounces: "Odd-numbered interstate highways go north and south, even-numbered east and west. The numbers get bigger from west to east and south to north."

"Well, now we know," Stephen says dryly.

A slow whine builds into a wail as Melanie wakes and feels hot, dry, and cramped all at once. "We're not there yet?"

"If you want to be a family man," Adam murmurs, "there's nothin' to have but kids."

Marian's own spirits lift in the presence of this, the old Adam that had been buried under the layers of pain, anger, and radiation burns for so many months now. She remembers their first confrontation after the doctors' casual "no hope" brought down the house of cards everyone had so carefully built up during the early stages of his illness. Her own furtive search for meaning collided with Adam's wall of denial. She'd pushed him. He had been so quiet all evening, not himself at all. While showering, Marian reviewed the facts and decided to talk to him, try to draw him out. He had been sitting on the edge of their bed, and didn't even speak when she slipped on a robe and began chatting with him while drying her hair.

"Adam, it's okay to talk to me about it. It's not just happening to you, you know, it's happening to all of us. To me."

"What's to say? I have cancer. A lot of people have cancer. Why should I be special?" His words were a dull thud, devoid of emotion.

"You have to wonder . . ."

"Why me? Marian, that sounds so cheap. Why anybody?"

"No, not just why you, but why this, why now, why everything. I don't have the answers, but . . ."

"Then why constantly ask the question!" He had spun around and slapped the wall with his open hand. Exhausted by his own rage and embarrassed by the quick tears, he had turned his back to the same wall and slid down to the floor, covering his face with both hands.

Stunned, she could only ask dumbly, inanely, "Did you hurt your hand?"

"God, Marian, I've got cancer. And you're worrying about my hand."

Kneeling beside him, she'd touched her own open palm to his and it was almost as if she could feel the sting of the angry slap in her own flesh. And they began to laugh, softly, tears still wet on both their faces.

"Don't laugh at me," the old clown had said, "it only eggs me on."

She kissed his forehead, pale and moist with the illness and the emotion. And kissed the angry red radiation lines drawn on the side of his face and neck and the smoky gray burned flesh within them. And, kneeling beside him, opened her robe and pressed his head to her bare breast. He had responded; he always responds. And asked her—he always asks her— "Marian, am I hot?" And touched his own wet index finger to his chest. She could feel his ribs move in a silent chuckle.

"Yeah, Adam, you're hot." Yet she had felt warm tears slide down over her hand still cupping his cheek. Maybe she had never loved him before; she loved him then.

She cradled him for what seemed like hours afterwards. "I barely know how to live, Marian," he'd whispered. "I don't know how to die."

They talked for hours; favorite things, secret fears. Like courting teenagers.

"I make it sound like dying is a special skill. I don't suppose you have to be terribly talented."

"Adam . . ."

"It's just that I feel like I should *do* something; but I don't know whether to write a great book, paint the sunset, or teach you how to change the oil in the car," and without waiting for a response, "You know, scientists say your body makes its own morphine for a mortal type pain; endorphins, I think they call them. Dying grace."

Now passion of any physical kind at all is out of the question, though there have been moments of great emotional sweetness very like it. "I feel like I'm getting ready to go home, back to where I came from; that's what slowly dying feels like, Marian, if anybody wants to know." She can't remember what she answered, only their sense of awe, almost peace. They could only absorb so much fear and dread and then it began to dissolve into this false peace, the superficial "high" of pressing on daily in the face of disaster. She remembers accounts of British citizens during World War II. The constant bombings and threats of bombings had eventually canceled out their terror and become like a public fireworks display: "Oh, look at that one." Even terror has a saturation point.

"I wouldn't know how to die either, Adam," she'd whispered, rocking his body ever so gently like an exhausted baby.

"From the time we understand birth we understand we will die. Every single one of us."

"Yes."

"And yet, like William Saroyan, I had always hoped that in my case an exception would be made."

South of Alice the landmarks turn to Spanish names: Encino, San Manuel, Rio Seco. The small tangles of converged traffic are not from shopping malls but from various weekend livestock auctions and fruit markets; the possums that Adam claims are born dead by the side of the road are joined by an occasional coyote cousin, not as wily as the ranchers' trucks. Bradley even spots a mangled javelina that didn't make it either.

The evidence of Christmas seems incongruous among the greenery and the balmy breeze. No real winter this, so the plastic nativity scenes and faded tinsel of the small towns look like relics that the owners were too lazy to remove. Even the geometric groves of oranges and other citrus look like imitation Christmas trees, the orange fruit hanging like glass balls before they are strung with lights. They had never been to the Valley at Christmastime before and they are all quiet, undecided whether the strange warm day and flat land are a disappointment or a reprieve after the cold but familiar "white Christmas" of home.

"Guess this means we're not gonna roast our chestnuts this year, huh," Bradley sums up their feelings.

. . .

When Marian was a little girl each Christmas had meant a renewal of hope that her father would come. Once, only a couple of years after that last dim departure, he had shown up with a present. It had been a cheap plastic doll in an outrageous pink dress, the kind she would have loved a few years earlier. She can't remember now how old she must have been then, but old enough to know the doll was cheap and not appropriate to her age. She had hugged him, thanked him, and never seen him again. Each year the hope that he would come again had faded, withered into a dim dream. There is still always something sad about the holidays to her, the brave little glimmer of the lights and tinsel just a false hope.

Any hope now, of course, is false. "Leave room for God to act," Michael had urged her in spite of the doctors.

"But He won't. Or doesn't. Which is worse?"

"We always want to account for every little detail of our prayers, right up to the results. We want a benevolent grandfather who wants to see us have a good time at his expense. Let the gap be. Let Him have the gap. Believe."

"There's too many mysteries."

Michael had smiled some secret amusement. "Don't you have adolescent boys?"

"Yes."

"And you remember your own adolescence?"

"Only too well."

"It was all a mystery, wasn't it? But the details that were so confusing then are laughably simple now, aren't they? Experience answered most of them. The things your own boys are in torment about now seem simplicity itself to us. Because we've lived them out. And I say that there is an expert spiritual simplicity, too, won by the living out of it every day. If you study doubt, you'll reap doubt. But faith answers its own mysteries."

"You'd be surprised what I really believe," Marian had said, defensive.

"I'm sure I would." Gently; oh so gently.

She rarely thinks about the mysteries anymore; the surprises take up all her time. They finally pull into a Dairy Queen for a late lunch. There is a derelict-looking old man drinking coffee and pacing nervously, looking out the window, then out the door. They all eye him nervously, keeping track of his odd behavior. After he finally leaves, the children buzz.

"That guy was weird!" Bradley begins.

"Yeah," Marian agrees. "I thought he was the sort we should keep an eye on. You never know what somebody like that might do."

By the time they finish their lunch the old man has been built up into a serial murderer on the ten-most-wanted list. They collapse into laughter when, as they pull out, Adam points out the reason for the old man's nervous concern. He has a pet coyote tied to the rusty bumper of his old pickup truck. They watch, Bradley and Melanie squealing, Stephen overcome with awe, as the old man gives the animal the scraps he has brought it from his lunch and gently untangles the rope it has fretted into a snarl.

"Well, we're home!" Adam laughs.

"Awesome," Bradley repeats over and over. "Can we get one, Dad?"

The children talk more, Adam and Marian less, as they turn off the main highway onto the back roads to Blake's farm. All day they've seen the beautiful spreads with cattle fencing and ostentatious gateways, presumably what Blake and Margaret had dreamed of. These back roads display many smaller versions, more nearly what they had ended up with. Numb with the hours and the flat terrain, Marian nearly misses Blake's road, skidding to a long, dusty halt in the loose caliche.

"Roll out, roll out!" Bradley springs into action, "four MIG's at three o'clock. Grab some leaves, we're goin' in under their radar!"

"Bradley," Melanie whines, shoving him away with her elbows.

"Mom," Stephen begins to protest, his face the ever-patient martyr.

"Relax," Marian interrupts, "we're here. We can all get out in a second."

The Stauffer farm does still claim its own name, "La Esperanza," swinging above its drive, rusty now, the gate permanently propped open. Once landscaped with specimen palms and the shocking purple of Convent bougainvillea, the entrance is now only a scraggly mess of errant branching stems and an occasional struggling bloom. The long driveway is still dusty caliche. Their own cloud of dust escorts them up to the house.

"Adam?" Marian notices the color has left his face again, a veil of light perspiration giving it a new sheen.

"I'm okay," he insists, "just a long day."

His voice is so thin and quavering that Marian is afraid he is going to cry. But the spell is broken in the flurry of the children piling out when they spot Fina coming out of the house. "Shall we sit here a minute?"

There's never an end to it, never even a moment to let down. Driving in and turning off the ignition should have brought relief. They'd made it, she had made the terrible drive and they were here! She should have at least a minute of relief, of victory. But no, those minutes are gone from her life now. She pushes her tired body on into the necessities. Like when she was little and she and her mother learned to do the things her father had taken care of before. Every small victory had been stolen by her mother's anger. He should have been there, he should help, he should send money. Never mind that Marian had done well enough, or that everything was all right. He should have been there. But she mustn't be angry with Adam; he can't help being sick.

"Adam! Señora!" Fina embraces them and touches each child, calling them by name and remarking on each in Spanish. Her eyes never show her feelings about Adam, but she has him in the house, on the couch with a glass of iced tea, before the rest of them can even get organized. By then Blake is answering their commotion with his own as the dogs greet his battered old pickup and cloud of dust.

"Granddad!" Melanie's cry is the first.

"Hey, Pop!" Bradley adds, hand extended for the distant handshake he knows Blake will offer.

Only Stephen actually approaches Blake in the middle of the tangle of dogs, patting his shoulder companionably. Blake responds in kind and Marian notices for the first time that they are very nearly the same height. "New dogs, Granddad?"

"Well, we knew old Chula would be dyin' soon, so we got this yellah pup here for her to train before she left us. She trained her all right. Darn fool dog acts like she's old, blind, deaf, and arthritic!" With one firm hand Blake keeps the bigger dogs down from Melanie while they talk. "Then 'fore she even turned a year old she went off and got herself in trouble with old Ben, the pointer next door. This here black one is the last of that surprise brood. The rest were pointers like Macho here. I'm training him for huntin'."

"He'll be mine, Granddad." Melanie already has the smallest black dog in her grip. No one argues. She'd had to leave her hamsters ("Simon and Simon" so she wouldn't get them mixed up) with neighbors back home; Marian doesn't have the heart to interfere now. The pup's back legs dangle helplessly beneath its swollen puppy-belly and Melanie's tight grip.

"Well, that takes care of Mellie's entertainment," Marian laughs. "Hello, Blake."

12

The week before Christmas was clear and mild, the days almost balmy, the nights chilly, Adam well enough to sit on the porch with Blake every afternoon. Fina brought girls from the neighboring houses and great mounds of masa to make tamales. The steaming pots of soaking corn husks filled the house with warmth and the women filled it with Spanish chatter. Simmering chickens hunched naked, breast down in huge pots, waiting their turn to be shredded with the chile powder and other mysterious ingredients. Fina showed Marian how to spread the pasty masa on a husk, press it thin with the little tortilla press, fill it, and fold it. She became a part of the busy little production line that turned out dozens of the delicious, greasy little treats, including a few of raisin and cinnamon for the children. Adam, whose appetite had been so poor for months, ate at least a dozen himself.

"I've always sort of hated Christmas, you know," Marian confided to Adam as she worked. "But this is fun."

"Hated Christmas?" he cried in mock horror. "Do you have

any idea where Dante says they put people who hate Christmas?"

Now, the first Saturday since the holidays, they are touring Adam's old haunts down by the river. "My roots," Adam winks at the boys as they round the last curve, through the tiny town of Madero. The "Lucky 5 Drive Thru" boasts a tiny dance floor outside under the hackberries. Next door is "Emma's Fireworks—No Smoking," a phenomenon Bradley can't resist. He has them take nearly a dozen pictures of himself and all of them together to send back home. And then Jose A. Cavazos's grocery store, the last chance to tank up before the river road and levees: a single regular gas pump and "Winston—Lo Tiene Todo" sign outside, a picture of the 1942 baseball team inside, along with the ubiquitous basket of green limes. The fine layer of dust speaks to the turnover rate; Marian spots thirty-nine-cent packs of sewing machine needles and Stephen, twenty-nine-cent shoelaces. "This is the oldest soda I ever drank," Bradley notes with awe.

"What is this stuff?" Stephen leans over a glass case full of some sort of chips.

"Chicharrones," Adam answers. "Fresh fried pork rinds."

"As in pig skin?" Bradley is really impressed now.

"Gross!" Melanie dismisses them all, sucking her bottle of Big Red.

"There's a place on the river where this old guy used to make 'em up fresh for us boys all the time. He died, I think."

"Yeah. Of heartburn."

Adam can't get over all the new "clubs" down on the river. "We were just innocent boys," he assures the kids. "We actually came down here to fish." Some of these look like good places to get knifed on a Saturday night.

"Mr. Cavazos's store was the closest cold drink, and all

that was here was that boat ramp. We even brought our own lights if we were going to fish at night." Adam takes such obvious pleasure showing it all to them that for a while it seems they are just another tourist family, taking in the local color. Bradley has them take his picture again under the "WARNING Tick Eradication Quarantine Line" sign. Then Stephen. And even Melanie by that time.

With the exception of the slower pace they keep for Adam's sake, it is like any happy family outing. They have the little oxygen tank, but only for security. They find a good shady spot near a shallow part of the river to eat lunch. Then while Adam dozes, Marian and Melanie explore the river's edge while the boys go down the road. They find a shallow, narrow place where Melanie can wade; could nearly wade across the entire river to the Mexico side, the water is so low and the sandy shores so high at the turn.

They are soon joined by other picnickers. A large Mexican family sets up nearby, the mother, very fat, installing herself on a partly submerged log as the many little ones strike out swimming and wrestling. The father and grandmother stay on the bank preparing the barbecue pit and arranging the food. The mother seems to have been there forever. Never moving, she controls her unruly brood with wild gesticulations and threats.

They haven't been there long when the smallest boy has his nose bloodied by the roughhousing, the shocking red blood on his bare chest as riveting as his screams. Still the mother never budges from her spot, only reels him in to her, cradling him in one corpulent arm while rinsing his face, chest, and the spurting fountain of his nose with the other hand. She croons to him and sways, all part of the rhythmic play, the bloody pantomime. No one moves a muscle toward a more compli-cated resolution. The child bleeds, the mother washes it away; he bleeds, she washes. A corpulent but tender pieta. She inter-rupts the tender cleansing and crooning only to heap Spanish vituperatives upon the rest of the brown tangle of arms and legs and young bodies. Two are eventually relegated to the bank with her omnipotent finger. The rest grind down into a more subdued swirl. Still the small bleeding boy lies across her lap, the blood now only a thin pink rinse down his face with each handful of river water the mother pours over him.

Marian, transfixed by the whole spectacle, looks down at her own white legs and wonders if the boy's blood swirls and eddies around her own naked legs there in the shallow, muddy water. Even Melanie is awed and stands clinging to Marian's side like a frightened monkey.

Still, there is something so comforting about it. So peaceful. If she could only hold Adam so now; drape him across her lap and gently submerge him in the river, rinse this ugly illness from him like that mother had done. So simple it seems; a bloody but tranquil baptism.

On the way home everyone sleeps like they are drugged while Marian guesses her way back to the main road, the land-marks she had noted on the way down to the river nearly use-less. She had especially marked one little frame house with one whole wall painted purple, but it has long ceased to be distinc-tive; every tiny frame house boasts its own brightly colored wall. They dot the brown landscape like so many Easter eggs. Early crops are in many of the fields, hygeria grain already grown up for windbreaks. The Our Lady of Fatima Catholic Church assures them that God loves them. The whole scene is peace itself and Marian almost believes it.

. . .

January brings the routine of the school days and the only really cold weather of the year. Adam's strength fails so rapidly that even Blake seems frightened and their peace is broken forever. They rent a hospital bed for Adam and move a cot into the little bedroom for Marian, leaving barely any room for their other things. In spite of the cheery quilts and bright new curtains for the wall of windows, the hospital bed overpowers the tiny room with its cold necessity. Until now it has been possible to go to bed at night pretending they are any married couple turning in for the night. Or just visiting.

Their lives become a round of blood tests and scares and disappointments again. Because there is no snow, the children worry and joke that maybe there won't be a spring. But February is like spring already, the air warmer, the few leaves that had disappeared in December already reappearing in new fresh green. The afternoon sun dapples the quilt on Adam's bed. The bed is pushed up close to the open window; Adam always wants to be where he can look out. Marian, sitting at Adam's bedside embroidering, wonders if the air might be too much for him, but she hates to break the easy silence, the first of a tiring day. The doctor had wanted to admit Adam to the hospital when the lab results were in, but Adam had begged to go home. They all know he'll eventually go in for more transfusions and breathing treatments, but have declared a truce for now. His color isn't good, and he is so emotional that Marian is afraid that his blood gases might be affecting his consciousness. But he was able to sit up an hour this afternoon and write in his journal and read some articles. She'll just wait and see.

"I loved my mother very much," Adam muses, staring at the

few remaining touches of her needlework and femininity left in this back bedroom. "But I think I hated her too." Even the crocheted afghan spread over his lap was Margaret's. He runs his fingers, thin and trembly now, over the scalloped edges.

"Why do you say that?" Marian is surprised, even though little of Adam's emotional musings surprises her anymore. She drops her own needlework in her lap to give Adam her full attention.

"She was the one I loved, trusted. But even she had this idea of me that was more important than I was. The 'only son' syndrome. I've always felt that I was sacrificed to that idea, somehow."

"Well, I imagine she did a lot of things just to protect their marriage. Your father was a difficult man."

"He was just as difficult to be a son to."

This plaintive quality of Adam's voice unnerves her; she's been surprised how much better this visit has been than she had imagined it would be. "You have to admit, Blake's gone out of his way to make us comfortable."

Adam continues as if he hasn't heard her. "She knew. Mother knew. She could have saved me, defended me. She chose him." He remembers her as a docile, pained animal turning away while Blake ground down the happy innocence of his childhood. "I guess part of me always expected her to rescue us both."

"Well, now, that strikes a chord. I know I always thought it was my mother's fault that my father left. Any time we disagreed I thought to myself, 'I bet that's why Daddy left.' Isn't that something? Why wouldn't I blame him for leaving? I was just like some barroom cowgirl accusing another woman of stealing her man, and all of the time the sorry son-of-a-gun is sitting right there, red-handed and lovin' it. Anyway, there's not really any comparison. Your father's different, but he's always done the right thing by everyone in his own way."

"If his own way just hadn't been the only way . . ."

Marian drops her needlework by the chair and goes to lower the window. She is always surprised at the distance, the flat horizon drawing her eyes away from the close little room. She turns and sits on the side of Adam's bed, pushing back the ever-encroaching pile of books, magazines, and notebooks around him. His hair is beginning to come back in now that they've quit the chemotherapy; she combs it back with her fingers while she listens to his heavy breathing. It is a moment not unlike the many she has spent with sick children, trying to settle their fevered restlessness with her own calm.

"I remember when your mother had her stroke and Blake kept her here at home after she got out of the hospital in spite of everyone's advice to the contrary. She was so terrified of going to a nursing home. Remember? He carried her around like a baby, kept her up in a chair near him when he was home."

"They loved each other; that always came first." He turns to her with a hint of the old twinkle. "Do you love me, Marian?"

"You know I do."

"That always comes first."

The peaceful moment is broken by Adam's squeezing cough, a constant companion now. It unnerves them both that he still holds the handful of tissues she offers him to his mouth, while most of the stringy mucus is propelled through the still-unhealed slit in his throat where the respirator had been attached. Before she can correct his aim he has ruined the front of his pajamas and sent himself into a purple rage of despair and hypoxia. Fina, always nearby, runs in to help Adam sit up where he can breathe easier. Marian uncurls the tubing to the little portable oxygen tank they keep handy now and brings it closer.

When he recovers enough to look over and see it there he nods his assent and she slips the green vinyl tubing into his nostrils, then wraps the rest around Adam's ears, culminating in a snug little noose under his chin. Almost in the same moment Fina has a crisp new pajama top on him and has disappeared with the soiled linens and litter from the bedside, murmuring constantly, slipping back and forth between a fluid Spanish and more halting English. Marian waits, her own breath halting and uncertain, for Adam to settle.

"Adam, are you comfortable now?"

He nods, wiping the corners of his eyes with a tissue.

"Do you need a pain pill?"

He nods his head yes, then no, then stares out the window reflectively a moment. "No, I don't think so. Not yet."

"Okay, but please remember what Dr. Guerra said about staying on top of the pain. Don't let it get ahead of you, Adam. It's all right to take the pain pills."

"I just don't like the way they make me feel, and then I sleep all day and get my days and nights mixed up. But I'll tell you when. Promise."

"Okay, then. Just rest." She sits down and takes up her needlework again. "That Fina is a wonder, isn't she? The best nursing care we've ever had! She probably already has those linens in the washer. I felt a little uncomfortable at first, being waited on, but she makes it seem like she's been hanging around, bored to tears, and just grateful that we've brought some entertainment."

"I know what you mean." His voice is huskier but seems all right. "When I was a boy, I worried about what she did all day while I was away at school."

"I bet." Marian irons the fresh cotton sleeve of Adam's pajamas with her hand, part caress, part orderliness. "What does she talk to you about? The English that I catch seems to be questions or answers to the Spanish monologues that I don't catch."

"Sermons."

"What?" thinking she has misunderstood.

"Little sermons. 'Leave it, leave it. God will take care of everything . . . help him, Virgin,' stuff like that."

"Really? I would have guessed it had to do with the linens. They didn't sound like words of comfort so much as facts."

"They are facts, to her. She asks God what He's up to, all right, but not like she expects an answer. The kind of stuff we hear on television that is so offensive in English."

These daily parades of crisis and near-panic are their life now. She knows they will come, but never accepts them, always fights. Always afraid the worst will happen. She remembers the same fear as a child, that the worst would happen. Then it did. She just wishes she could have remembered him, the family, the way they had been at Christmas. At peace.

Now there is no peace. Stephen is the only one of the children who seems to like it here. Melanie is whinier every day because her mother has so little time for her; Bradley is so homesick that his usual breezy personality is wilting. Adam's few fitful hours of sleep that only come with desperation are not peaceful. Marian has forgotten what peaceful would be like. She remembers the peace of their lives before; even the pills she had battled years ago hold out a kind of peace. She remembers the way they had nibbled at the edges, blunting them, blurring the lines until her life and all its ragged circumstances were like a soft watercolor instead of the sharp, jangling edges of the art they called modern and nonobjective. A sentimental Rockwell with a puppy in the corner with a bandaged paw. The other people she had met during her two weeks at the chic, elegant Hellmann Center reeked of that same sentimental preference and she had learned to recognize its aroma. It would be a simple matter to have one of Adam's doctors write her a prescription; anyone in her position would be under stress; they would realize that.

But no. Some things, as Adam says, even a low-fat diet and Xanax won't cure. They would go on, with peace or without it. Dispensable, this peace, it seems, just like hope.

Adam turns on his side as if to nap, but after several minutes she can see that his lashes are wet with tears as he stares out into the flat horizon. Dropping the needlework that would not bend itself to her fingers anyway, she lies down beside him, fitting her body to his broad back. He never says a word and she cannot hear him crying. But, lightly rubbing the smooth cotton of the fresh pajamas she can feel the jagged efforts to control his breathing, can almost feel the deep misery that has overcome him.

"Sh-h-h," she whispers to him as she strokes his back and arm. "Sh-h-h," just as she always had with the children, comforting them from some illness or deep sorrow. And the thought comes to her, as it often did when she was caring for them, that she would take the suffering into her own body if she could. Or share it. Or put her own strength into them somehow; share her very substance with them. She has always thought of Adam as her strength. She would be his now, if she only could. But she can only softly rock him. Rock him like a baby and whisper "sh-h-h."

13

All during January Stephen and Blake worked with Macho, Blake's pointer. Blake tied an old, dry quail wing to the end of a reel of light nylon fishing line and they threw it out and worked it slowly, teasing Macho into the point that he knew by instinct. The dog already knew the basics: sit, stay, simple fetching. They fired over his head at feeding time and did some target practice to make sure the pup wouldn't be gun shy. It was just a matter of capitalizing on his instincts and keen sense of smell—teach him to find coveys of quail, point them, hold the point until the gunner came up behind him, then flush them into flight to be picked off. Dog's instincts and hunters' necessities woven into a pattern that would please both.

Now, late in February, they are out in the brush to put all the lessons together in the field before the season is over. Hunters and dog come to do the thing the dog was born to and they have all worked toward for months—find the quail and shoot them. Blake carries his old 12-gauge shotgun cradled in the crook of his left arm, stock resting on his hip. Stephen, who didn't want to tell his grandfather that he had never shot anything but a paper target before, copies him, matching every detail of posture with his own lighter 20-gauge, a Christmas present from Blake.

Macho, for his part, is a leaping, twisting, shivering blur of nervous sniffing and snorting in the dusty mounds of bushes. Stephen lifts Macho's water bowl down and fills it from an old plastic jug.

"Shells?" Blake asks, patting his hunting vest and looking back at Stephen.

"A whole box, Granddad." Stephen has already checked and double-checked. He is as excited as Macho but tries to force himself to move slowly and talk calmly. The rubber-lined bird pouch on the back of his vest is already making his back sweat. He can't believe it's this hot in February. He loves it; feels that the heat has thawed out something in him long frozen. He is not so awkward here, so cautious. And talking, never his strong suit, isn't much called for in his grandfather's company. In fact, he's noticed that the less he talks the more his grandfather talks. As long as he doesn't look at him. It seems that what Blake has wanted is an audience, not a conversation. They understand each other perfectly.

They push out through the thick weeds, circle around the clumps of cactus, then make easier headway on flat, dry patches of dirt. "Find the birds," Blake speaks firmly to Macho, gesticulating dramatically with his long arm. "Go find the birds."

It is all Macho has been waiting for and he takes off in a zigzag version of the direction Blake has already established for them, darting from clump to clump of weeds and bushes, sniffing, snorting, occasionally raising his head to smell the wind and redirect his search. They have to maintain a pretty fast pace to keep up with him, but Blake doesn't call him in.

"He's an ideal quail dog," Blake laughs, slightly winded already. "All heart." Finally he is forced to call Macho in, rest a bit, send him out again, and try to slow his pace with his own calm demeanor. Now Macho begins to act more businesslike. His body becomes tenser, moves in slower, tighter patterns. Then Blake and Stephen both sense that there is a change; the dog is onto something.

"When he goes on point now," Blake whispers back to Stephen, "you've got to walk in fast behind him. He won't hold it long, so be ready for the flush. Focus on the sky where the birds will be and get ready to shoot."

Stephen heightens the tension in his already alert stance, eases the safety off his gun. He tries to imagine what the covey will look like as it leaves the ground, just which direction it will take.

"He's young and inexperienced, so he's liable to break and chase a flush. Just be careful, don't shoot too close over his head." Blake's instructions are a whispered monologue issued while they tramp stealthily through the long grass. He stares straight ahead and never turns to look at his gangly grandson suddenly grown graceful and alert, trudging close behind him.

"You take the first shot, Granddad." There are things Stephen suddenly isn't sure of: how long to wait, how high to aim, whether to kneel down.

But Blake signals to him to come up beside him and pantomimes the whole scenario to come, right down to the slight kneeling position when he shoots, then whispers, "You take it, son. You can do it." They both know, from Macho's determined tension, that the moment is near.

"The distance will be good. Don't fail to shoot thinking it's too far." His whispered instructions are a steady quiet drumbeat now. "Stay here, now . . ." And then, in ecstasy: "There! His first solid point!" The dog is frozen in a mass of bridled energy, as if every muscle in his body opposes every other one, like the quivering inertia of arm-wrestling.

The next moments are a slow blur, a telescoping of time and action into frozen frames that will remain in Stephen's mind as some of the happiest, most satisfying of his eighteen years. The dog and the gun and his own tense body all do what they have been prepared to do, and work together flawlessly, if only for those few seconds. Even the quail seem to rush willingly into their destiny. Stephen sights one and drops it with his first shot. The rest is confusion as the other quail scatter, Macho runs to Blake, and Stephen goes for the bird himself, running. Until Blake calls him back.

"Hold up, son."

Stephen freezes and Blake advances with Macho to look for the bird. Blake advances, training the dog to retrieve the bird.

"We've exercised his muscle, now we've got to exercise his mind." Blake is clearly winded now, and Stephen runs up to take the 12-gauge from him, leave his hands free to work with Macho. "Come on, boy, find the bird."

Stephen wants to stop everything and throw his arms around Macho and run find the dropped bird himself. Give a yell, maybe, and do a little jig. But for Blake, it is business as usual until the dog delivers the bird he should have kept his eye on all along.

Finally that one blessed bird ends up, headless, in the little pouch on Stephen's back. Before the morning is over, it is joined by two others. Blake's side pouch has two or three as well, Stephen loses count. But he is very sure of his three, a heavy little lump there on his back, still warm. It is the happiest day of his life.

By the time they work their way around the field and back to the pickup, even Macho has lost his pep. His head hangs low to the ground where his sniffing becomes increasingly desultory. He develops an odd little trot that seems to barely require his feet to leave the ground. Blake and Stephen are drenched in sweat and coated with a fine layer of dust.

"He's a great dog, Granddad."

"Anyway, now we know he'll cut that brush into ribbons looking for quail," Blake agreed, obviously pleased. "Just needs some work on the retrieving."

"Is that a problem?"

"Nah. You can teach near any dog to retrieve. What we just did was the tricky part."

After his floppy tongue devours most of the water in his bowl, Macho splashes his front paw in the rest to wet himself and flops down in the cooler dirt under the tailgate, panting.

Blake and Stephen empty their guns and store them carefully in their long cases, then pull the ice chest out to have their cold drinks. Stephen puts two old lawn chairs under the shade of some huisache trees so they can rest while they finish their drinks and clean the birds before heading back.

"You skin 'em, just like a rabbit," Blake demonstrates on the first quail, pulling the skin over the body, feathers and all, to reveal the white meat underneath. "Take these shears and clip the wings and feet and tail, then cut down both sides of the backbone." It is all one smooth motion as he talks, ending with a tidy little carcass which he rinses thoroughly with water from the plastic jugs.

"They stink," Stephen observes, surprised.

"Yeah, quail do. That's why you have to clean 'em up and rinse 'em real good out in the field. We'll wash 'em again under the faucet when we get back with 'em."

They work on in silence, Stephen skinning them and handing them to his grandfather. Then Blake hands the shears to Stephen and busies himself rinsing and storing the first small group. Macho pants heavily still, moving only to stretch and find a cooler spot of dirt.

"You're sure good with dogs, Granddad." Stephen keeps his eyes down on the bird he is working on, careful to cut exactly as he has seen Blake do it, satisfied to see the carcass come clean on the first try.

"Better than with people, I expect." There is no sign of humor in his remark.

"Macho was great."

"Might be good as old Belle was." Blake stands, looking out into the distance, the bloody rinse water dripping from the handful of cleaned birds. "Now there was a great dog. If you didn't have your limit by noon there just weren't any birds flyin'."

Stephen hands Blake the carcass he has finished; still they never look at each other.

"When she died, I put my guns away, wasn't going to hunt any more. At my age, figured it was time to retire anyway. Truth is, I didn't really want to invest in another dog; every one takes part of you, don't think it doesn't. Just like kids." His eyes turn hooded and he nods in agreement with some inner memory or pain.

"Then old ChaChi presented me with that litter of five little spotted surprises." He laughs at the memory. "I thought maybe surprise was the very thing I needed. I figured I could train this one last one. We'll close out our last season together; he'll be the only one I never had to bury."

They work together quietly, finishing the birds and putting them away in a plastic bag in the ice chest.

"They were born the same day I got the call about your Dad."

[ADAM'S JOURNAL]

March 10:

Bittersweet satisfaction to watch my father give my oldest son the very thing I could never give him—a sense of himself and his place in things. I never knew what he lacked; knowing it, even, would probably not have been able to give it. Loving him, I am glad for him to have it.

"God is satisfied with you," Michael told me once. "At the moment you accept that, you become His glory and honor and crown." It is something to roll the right lobe of my brain around anyway. There's no question of my performance, now, you know; I can neither toil nor spin. But glory? Yes, I could believe in glory. And honor? Oh, yes; to leave this pale life behind me in honor, just a friendly, clean Norman Rockwell painting, me, the kids, the dogs, the warm ground here, dry and dusty on top, damp and sensuous where the dogs turn over new berths for themselves in the shade. But I have listened for this quiet voice of assurance everywhere since and cannot make it out.

The honeyed words made perfect sense to me in the ICU's foggy stupor. I listen to the TV evangelists with their expensive suits and pompadours ("would Jesus wear a Rolex?") but the sonorous elocution is not for me. It's for someone, plainly—their results are chalked up on giant boards like a mega-telethon.

March 25:

I'm still all here, but pruned down to the essentials; the tiniest representation of myself. Anyone can take me in at a glance. A Bonsai. Now that it's too late, I know what it was I wanted to do with my life: sing and give talks. Yes, that's it; what really gives me satisfaction is to hear my own erudite words. If I could just prolong them, round them out with pear-shaped notes filled with emotion. Then people would listen. Then I could tell them . . . what? Little boats of story or song, each set afloat with a tiny gem, a hard stone of Truth. Myself, spotlighted on a dark stage; the curtain falls away. I see the people I love; they are like snowflakes, each beautiful, each different. And they see me as I am. The Truth, once we all see it, will seem self-evident.

surrender=peace

control=anxiety

Pascal: "If I had not known You, I could never have found You."

Rule #1: "Don't sweat the small stuff."
Rule #2: "It's all small stuff."

What has my life been, that I am so unwilling to lose it? Mowing the grass, waxing the car, working sixty hours a week under buzzing fluorescent lights that give me a headache. It seems like the most blessed, the most precious of lives to me now. So impossible to leave that I hear myself moan and they ask me if it is the pain. Yes, it is the pain. Tearing myself from what I know so well . . . for what? I dream long, dark, running dreams with no destination, no arrival. I always wake before the arrival. Oh, to have been old and finished, so familiar with this scent that I wouldn't have to sniff it again. Death.

God, I thank you for my life. And will not hold my dying against you, Hound of Heaven, Sir. Only what about all those PTA meetings, root canals, so many Rolaids after the precinct conventions? How many hours have I spent dipping the dogs, spraying the house, poisoning the ants? The only good news they ever have for me now is that I'm not dead yet. Thank you God for the people who love me and I forgive the ones who weren't too good at it. Sure enough, here at the end there is only love. And that amazing grace. I told the doctors that all I wanted was some warning before I died so I could get out of that place and come home to die. They never promised even that—these people are cold, don't even deal in dreams—but here I am. Wouldn't this be as good a time as any, Sir? To quit? When does the fat lady sing? Having been "dying" for so long now, I probably won't be satisfied until I do.

P.S. The Talk Radio doctor says a lack of sense of direction can be caused by calcification of the pineal gland.

That's it! I'm sure it is . . . everything's going to be fine, now!

Dear Michael:

I'm finally writing, as promised, but might beat my letter home, as they say from the European tour. We're down to the last inning in any case; "one day at a time," like an alcoholic. I imagine you have many new customers by now. Or are you gone? I'm afraid I have you fixed in my mind like a gerbil on a wheel, doing what you did for me over and over again for faceless strangers.

Seriously, though, I do miss our visits. Wish you were here now, in fact, to help me chop my way through this wild jungle of implausibilities. "This isn't even hardball, yet" you told me when I balked at your words. (God-Lite? I thought.)

My father and I have, indeed, reconciled in our timid ways, as you predicted. It's a relief to be right with him for once. In any case, I and my entire family are totally dependent on him now, so there's no use arguing! The very thing that kept me away from people like you was that my own family never talked about anything but God and hard work. I never wanted to hang out with Puritans; now here I am tied up in their compound.

Adam Stauffer

14

Marian watches the crowd gather at the Sheriff's Posse Arena; the milling people and restive animals raise a cloud of fine dust. It is already hot now in March, and the wind is just now, with the cooler air of evening, dying down from near gale force during the day. The roads out to the arena had been banked with mounds of huisache blossoms blown there like mounds of orange snow and there are stray drifts of them along the rough boards of the arena and under the open bleachers.

It's a far cry from a concert at Ravinia, but Marian has to admit it's exciting in a different sort of way. She thinks of the Chicago skyline, seen from the planetarium peninsula, and has a pang of homesickness. It is the first hour she has spent away from Adam's bedside. He had insisted that he would be fine there with Fina, and Raul was nearby if they needed anything. She had been reluctant, but knew it was a big day for the kids. Stephen would ride in his first event, Blake riding with the older men to keep things moving. Bradley and Melanie are wild with excitement at their first rodeo. And, Marian admits, it feels good to be only a spectator in this open space.

That's what this land seems to have the most of: space. Her first trip south with Adam years before, the long, lonely stretches of highway between towns had amazed her. And the monotony. The plains back home were rolling hills compared to this. There the little towns were separated primarily by their signs. Here she feels like she should fill a canteen; every town is an oasis. If Chicago is the windy city, then this whole toe of Texas is the land of the big sky, and she is glad for it now.

Back home they are just getting ready for Casimir Pulaski day and the whole area will be given over to the celebration of a Polish revolutionary war hero. Here the merchants are getting ready for the onslaught of shoppers from Mexico on "Semana Santa" vacation. There is a "fiesta" for everything: citrus and vegetables and crafts by the local Junior Service League ladies. You'd have to go to Warsaw to find a larger Polish population than Chicago, and you'd no doubt have to go to Mexico to find a more Mexican population than in the Valley. All foreign in their own American ways; Marian is growing accustomed to this flat, dusty, Tex-Mex world.

"Hey, Mom!"

Marian waves in the direction of Stephen's voice, but she can't quite make out which form is his, they all look so much alike in hats, plaid shirts, and well-worn jeans. Bradley and Melanie point him out before she locates him.

"Hey, Bucko!" Bradley yells. He is more like his father all the time, a clown even while pea-green with jealousy to see Stephen in the saddle.

"Mom, listen," Bradley drops down beside her, "some of

the guys want us to stop at the airfield on the way to the live-stock show next week." Always thinking, planning, whirling. Marian changes gears slowly.

"Why?"

"They've got these great models they fly out there. They're going to let me fly one."

"I don't think so, Bradley, not this time."

"Aw, Mom, why not? It won't take but an hour or two. There'll still be plenty of time at the livestock show."

"Because we'll have Melanie and her friends, too. They don't care about airplanes. You can go do that with your friends another time."

"Well, she can fly dolls or something. Come on, Mom." But she can tell he has already relented and is ready to move on to another deal.

Melanie scrambles up the wood slats of the fence to clear the top. "I see him, I see him!" She screams and waves until she hears the crowd titter at her little-girl enthusiasm. Her now-six-year-old bravado reminds Marian of her own as a child. Watching her deal with Adam's gradual withdrawal from their lives evokes Marian's own sense of abandonment as a child. The murky vision she'd always had of betrayal. Her father's? God's? Some huge, wrenching presence smashing her feelings until, like damaged radar, they were no longer reliable. She lives it over daily now with Melanie. So easily wounded, so slow to heal.

"Well, we may be a bunch of city slickers, Bradley, but I'd say your brother blends right in." There are many boys around Stephen's age, some younger, and some older. All canter by with the same insolent one-handed charioteer's grip and loose posture. Blake is talking to the group of older men watching the chutes, but he always notices when it's Stephen's turn to canter by, raising his right hand in what would be a half-hearted salute from anyone else. Coming from Blake it equals Melanie's enthusiasm.

"Boy, Granddad's really gettin' into this," Bradley says in admiration. Marian has noticed the same thing. Blake had taken extraordinary pains to clean up the old tack room and get the horse trailer fixed up. Most of his own horses were gone now, but Raul had brought up one of his own, and one someone had for sale. Blake said he didn't ride anymore, but he saddled one right alongside Stephen every day and sat it while he taught Stephen. Then in the evenings when he was through with his work Raul would take Stephen out across the fields riding for an hour or longer. When he'd disappeared after school every day one week they found out he was running barrels with a girl down the road who had her own horse.

Bradley had been the one to find out, of course. "Shame, shame, we know her name!" he'd teased Stephen at the dinner table.

"Who?" they'd all echoed in unison, not realizing who was the target this time.

"Cindy Smalling's new arch enemy, that's who," Bradley had offered.

"Oh?"

"Yeah, I found out why Stevie and Trigger all of a sudden outgrew the old pony corral."

"Bradley . . ." Marian stopped him out of sympathy for poor Stephen, whose fair complexion showed the rising blush like a high fever.

"His name's not Trigger, it's Poco," Melanie had insisted, with her usual grasp of the central issue.

"You shouldn't be following your brother around like that, Bradley. How would you like it if Melanie spied on you all the time?"

"I haven't been spying!" he had protested, with the indignant stridor of the guilty. "I heard him telling Dad about it."

Anyway, it's done now and Stephen is irrevocably in the saddle. "Is Stephen's girlfriend supposed to ride in this thing today, Bradley?" Marian wonders.

"Granddad said she was—barrel racing." His eyes constantly scan the riders in the arena and the sparse crowd. Marian knows if anything significant happens, Bradley will see it. She relaxes her own gaze and tries to get comfortable on the old wooden bleachers.

There is a steady parade of people back and forth. It seems to Marian as if the arena full of cocky boys is set in relief against the slow parade of dour old men ambling by, the insolence wiped off their leathery faces by the realities of life. The older, stooped, solemn ones give way to the younger ones leaning forward in their saddles, *Homo habilus* become *Homo erectus*.

Marian watches, barely breathing, while Stephen takes his turn at calf-roping. As far as she can tell, he looks as expert as anyone else and she begins to relax. She watches the bull riders and makes a mental note of gratitude to Blake for keeping him away from that ambition. In fact, she owes Blake a great debt on many counts concerning Stephen. She has never seen him so content. So sure of himself. As if he was born to the very life Blake had harbored here all these lonely years. The life Adam had escaped from. They hunted and they worked on the equipment in silent companionability. She has even heard them discussing building up a herd of Santa Gertrudis cattle, good cattle like Blake had aspired to owning when he was still trying to build his spread up into something to be proud of.

"Mom, look!" Bradley shrieks.

"What?" Marian knows it must be Stephen, follows Bradley's and Melanie's frantic gestures to the arena. She recognizes the familiar profile just in time to see it leave the saddle in a neat trajectory and connect—wham—with the ground at the right shoulder. For the long moment that Stephen is still, Marian is paralyzed; run? pray? scream? But before her muscles can organize a plan she sees Stephen roll over and sit up. Blake rides over and reaches down to help him up. The terror passes into elation. If tension and release is what makes Bach great, she remembers Adam saying, then mothers are famous somewhere.

Blake, dismounted by now, walks Stephen off to the first aid station. The thing that Marian wants most to do—run down to her son, supervise the medical attention he receives—she knows would be the worst thing she could do. Blake will tend to him. It is important that she keep her vigil in a quiet, distant way, broken bones or no.

Marian thinks of poor old Chula, one of Blake's dogs, who had wandered into the street the week before. They had found her as they drove back out after dinner in town, a tawny silhouette on her side, only the bloody smile giving her secret away. Her black pup stood vigil, mourning and sniffing at what he didn't understand. It was as if Chula had planned, even there at the violent end, to fall just far enough away from the traffic to keep her curious baby out of danger. As if she had known the pup would sniff and whine at her fur until Blake buried her under the twisted mesquite by the shed. As if she had known the pup would stand howling at the dark spot on the road all night and she had planned to keep him out of danger even in her own death.

Melanie had been the pup's only comfort, carrying him faithfully around every waking minute. She gave him the first name that stuck more than a few hours: Sorry. Adam had said it was the best possible name, that he'd always known the dog was sorry. Melanie had been pleased with herself and healed of her own grief.

Adam misses his own dogs and already has professions for the local ones. He says Sorry is a dyslexic track star, twenty-one, running barefoot in her first meet. Raul's old black Lab mix is a gentlemanly old Negro shoeshine man from downtown. Chula had been president of the ladies' garden club, a little stiff but kindly in her way. Marian thinks of her own little mutt she'd had when she married Adam. Prissy. She had been a prima ballerina, according to Adam, but had married for love, given up her career and grown fat. Eight years later Adam had held Prissy, blind and arthritic, while the vet put her to sleep. Marian had watched, hypnotized by the old dog's sleepy trust, as the milky eyes closed for the last time.

Marian has several bloody memories from the Valley now and wonders if it is the place or only her own mind-set. She thinks of the pristine little statue, "1956 Year of Mary Immaculate," at the park in La Lomita. Purest white plaster, simplest lines; yet at the feet a gaudy picture of Christ on the cross, blood running from head and hands and feet and side. Is it always women at the momentous bloody occasions? The fat woman at their river picnic washing her bloody little boy,

161

Mary herself, and now Marian leaning over Adam's tortured body; always the women. That day at La Lomita Marian had cried at the tiny white feet of the diminutive Mary, sorrowing eternally over the bloody remains of her beloved son. Cried for herself, lost, alone in a grief too long, a job too big for one woman.

"Mom," Bradley nudges her with his elbow. "Don't cry now, Mom. You haven't cried all day. You're on a roll!"

She knows he's right; she can have a day with the children, for heaven's sake, without getting morbid. Besides, Adam is stable; the doctor in town had done lab work last week.

"He was very complimentary about my platelets," was all Adam reported, one shaky hand still holding the cotton pad over the new wound in the crook of the opposite arm. Marian had always loved Adam's hands, large, the prominent veins snaking across them proudly, not too rough or too soft. Good, honest hands. Now they are Rodin's hands, twisted and poignant, the color no more real than the bronze ones.

"See you in two weeks." The doctor had said it so lightly. She took it as a reprieve; almost a guarantee. They would be there in two weeks. Still be there. And Adam wouldn't be forced to go in for more transfusions yet, the "vampire syndrome" he calls it, dependent on other people's blood.

"What you need," he had explained to the transfusion nurse, "is a chain letter: 'Squeeze out a little blood and send it to the name at the top of the list. In three weeks you should get 318 pints of blood. The one who breaks the chain gets AIDS.'"

Melanie shrieks, "There she is! Stephen's girlfriend," and waves wildly, knocking loose Marian's visor and her melancholy.

"Check these names, Mom," Bradley says, waving the program in front of her. "Why do they name their kids stuff like Jesus and Mary all the time? And 'Primitivo.' Gah, awesome . . . Primitive Gonzales! And Moron. Would you ever name a kid Moron? Even 'Pains.'"

"Pains?" she and Melanie ask in unison.

"Yeah. Dolores means 'pains.' I looked it up."

15

Marian is glad when the time comes to enter the little local hospital for the inevitable transfusions and treatments. It is like a vacation to be relieved of the daily grind of responsibility for Adam's care, the constant preoccupation with medications and oxygen level. It is so quiet and peaceful here that even Adam is content, calls the little rural hospital the Hiatus Regency. The huge hospital in Chicago always had them in rooms looking out onto concrete and asphalt from the dizzying perspective of the fifth or seventh floors. Here they are actually at ground level—the only level. The boys can bring Melanie right up to the window after school to satisfy her curiosity about Daddy's room.

The windows here look out on lawns of carpet grass and circles of Cocus plumosas—"ponytail palms" that did, indeed, look just like a pony's tail in the stiff southeast breeze—planted three per circle and filled in with bright multicolored petunias. Tall hedges of oleander, heavy with pale pink blossoms, block the view of the parking lot.

Adam is sicker than ever, but somehow seems more content. He writes in his journal when he can, sleeps a lot, sits staring out the window when they get him up twice a day. Now, while Adam sleeps, Marian sits in the big chair by the window herself, looking out at the flat, tropical landscape as she often sees Adam doing. What nature seems to have forgotten in the way of hills and trees is made up for in color, it seems to her. All winter there has been uninterrupted green: fields of carrots, dark green and lacy as fern, swaying palms, feathery mesquite. Now there are rows filled with purple cabbage, like giant dusky rose blossoms. And bright hibiscus of every hue snuggled against the houses, clumps of orange or yellow or even lavender lantana along fencelines, tall hedges of oleander with ever-present blossoms of pink or red or white. There are beds springing up everywhere of petunias and periwinkles and pansies of every color imaginable. The hospital lawn is already dotted with color. Relaxed, nearly napping, Marian's focus softens and she sees something she has never noticed before.

The large glass expanse of windows and the L-shaped solarium at the turn of the sidewalk conspire in a magical illusion. By some miracle of reflected light, the wing-shaped brick buttress of the exterior wall is rendered transparent. She can see the swaying palms and hackberries there, superimposed on the brick, in line with those far off at the other end of the sidewalk and those close up here by their room. Even the people coming and going on that outside sidewalk appear in reality at the far end, in shimmering apparition through the transparent brick, then again in solid reality at this near section of sidewalk. She sits and confirms the unlikely visual disruption of the solid brick reality over and over again, mesmerized. Could this be what Adam sees as he sits there, transfixed, every afternoon?

Marian's vision foreshortens as she gazes, insatiable, at the transparent brick wall. Then a variation of the same trick of light and glass gives her back her own reflection in the room's window. At first she denies the slack-jawed, middle-aged intruder, lifting her eyebrows at it in dismay. But it lifts its eyebrows back and she knows. Marian picks up her jaw, passes a hand over the disheveled hair, shifting some in the big chair to improve the posture. To no avail; she is that tired, middle-aged illusion.

She is surprised she even cares. It is an old score that has been settled by the competing richness and variety of married life and Adam's desire for her. She wanted, as a young woman, to be beautiful. The sixties, when she was a hippie like all the other college kids, suited her. She was pretty; never stylish. The flirtation with drugs dulled her ambition, diverted her interest. But still she had wanted something other than the hand she had been dealt by her plain, doe-eyed mother and shadowy father. Even as a mature woman whose husband found her so attractive, the hunger would not die.

"I wish I were beautiful," she remembers telling Adam once. "For you. I mean, I love you and I would like it if you could say you had a beautiful wife."

She cannot remember now what his answer had been; thinks it must have been swallowed up in a physical affirmation. She had been beautiful to him and it had been enough that he loved her. Still, something in her is dismayed to see the melting lines of her exhausted face in the reflection. Wistful to see her hands, knotty now with years of hot dishwater, carrying groceries, the daily working of the complicated dough of everyday family life.

"See my soul," she whispers. To herself; to no one in particular.

"I am older now and gravity does what it is sworn to do." She is firm with herself; practical.

Still, she wishes she were beautiful.

"See my soul," her hooded eyes say.

"See my beautiful, young, well-dressed soul."

The reflection nods in graceful admiration.

She hears Adam stir and turning, realizes he has been watching her.

"You're talking to yourself, Marian. Should I worry?"

"Not unless you heard me. Then I'll have to divorce you and move far away." She stands and tucks her blouse into her slacks and combs her hair with her fingers.

"Not a word, I swear." He moves up in the bed and the open book laid across his abdomen slips to the floor.

"I'll get it," Marian says, dashing over to recover the book. She holds it and, smoothing the jacket, recognizes it as one the auxiliary lady left for him. "Good book?"

Adam chuckles. "Nah. Just one of those pissin'-in-the-fire, macho cowboy books. Guess the little lady figured us good ol' Texas boys like 'em thataway."

She helps him push up in bed and straightens the tangled covers, careful of the plastic tubing filled with dark blood. None of it shocks her anymore; she barely thinks of the blood at all. She only raises her eyebrows in question at Adam's description of the book.

"These things are a genre of their own now, you know. A man's romance novel, really, with raw hides instead of ripped bodices. I've counted three rapes, two fistfights, one beating, two menstruations, and one live birth in the bushes." He takes the book and closes it firmly to set it aside. "And that's just the first chapter."

"Like you always say, Adam, there's just no future for you in Texas misogyny."

"Guess my mama was too nice to me. There could be money in it, though," he says, feigning a sudden reluctance to set it aside. "I can see it now: *Rawhide* by Danielle L'Amour."

She snatches the book from him and puts it at the bottom of his ever-present stack on the table. "At least it's better than the ones Mother is always giving me: *If We Can Walk on Water, Then We Can Do a Cartwheel* and such, usually by the Cosmic Church of Protoplasm or something . . ."

"*On the Brink With Charles Kuralt . . .*"

"Exactly."

"Hellooo," the nurse's aide calls out cheerfully as she wheels the blood pressure machine in. "Time for vital signs."

"I like it here," Adam says. "The only things they want from me are blood and vital signs. And they put the blood back."

"Good afternoon," the nurse calls out briskly.

"You don't want to help me with my coping skills, do you Miss Martinez?" he teases her.

"Sir?" Her expression is blank, uncomprehending.

"Or tell me how everything is just what you expected, huh, Miss Martinez?"

"No sir." She is sure of that part.

"Adam, don't tease," Marian chides him. "Listen, I'm outta here. If you're okay for now, I'm going to run home, check on the kids. I'll be back in an hour or so."

She gathers his soiled pajamas and the newspaper they've finished reading. "Anything else to send home, to cut down the clutter?"

"Sh-h-h, you're bothering Miss Martinez. She can't hear if my signs are vital enough."

"Adam . . ."

"Okay, okay. Bye."

As she gets to the door, Adam calls her back.

"Marian, how many therapists does it take to change a light bulb?" She gives him a look of impatience.

"Only one. But the bulb has to be willing to change."

[ADAM'S JOURNAL]

March 25

If you know not how to die, never trouble yourself; Nature will in a moment fully and sufficiently instruct you; she will exactly do that business for you; take you no care for it.—Montaigne

After having hid from it behind every available tree, I have now made death my friend. I see it—far off, or sometimes close up—with tender longing. It's the only thing left to do. Special. Like Marian feels about having our babies and nursing them: a new experience, not like anything else. Not half of a simile. And I see the world, manicuring its nails while its poor thin soul shivers in tatters. Death, in fact, gets to be beside the point; it's life that's so overwhelming. My body rots from the inside out like a dying tree, but something in me prospers. This puzzle that is death cannot be so personal, so intense; it is not rare. People do it all the time. And there's worse things than dying.

March 30

I found that passage Michael read to me in the hospital: "To him who overcomes, to him I will give some of the hidden manna, and I will give him a white stone, and a new name written on the stone which no one knows but he who receives it." I don't even understand it, but I want that white stone, and already call myself a name no one seems to recognize. No pat answer to a generic question, but a pure stone with my own secret name chiseled there by someone who knows me well. I, who have been so poor in spirit. Limping, broken, like Jacob, worn out from striving with God and man, I want a new name too. More than a new name; a new medium. It will hold the same fascination our videos of each other did when the camera was new. The same dogs and shelves and me in my underwear and Marian in her nightgown . . . all transformed into a fascinating docudrama holding us spellbound for hours.

I can remember being on the respirator, though, mercifully, through the gauze of a dream. Wild panic to be gagging, the slow realization that air was coming anyway. Then sinking, slowly, down, down to where I trusted that other power to breathe for me, never mind the trussed grin, dry and cracking. Even when we know there is something better, we hold onto what we know. Hang on, in fact, to any old ratty thing when it's what we know. This buried dinosaur of faith was there then, though I could not tell bone from stone. Some of it has taken shape with hammer and chisel, some lightly dusted clean with brushes. It is there now, I know, though I cannot see the shape of it.

P.S. What do those who don't overcome get? A pointed hat?

April 7

What if I repent in dust and ashes?

What was my life? With the doing cut from under me, I can see that I am not what I do. The quiet despair that haunted the places I carved out, the book I wanted to write and the sense that the world—God—didn't really need another book. But it—He—never really needed another baby either. One blood-red wing closes over me, terrible and glorious. The thing I would have made of my life had it been given me once more. Ashes to ashes, dust to dust. But what were my dreams made of? And where will they go?

April 10

Call me Ishmael, too.

April 15

Nothing works, nothing works. I make a fist to protest. It won't work, either.

Abort, Retry, Ignore?

16

Marian hears the noise in the hall outside Adam's room pick up as the hospital stirs with the chaos of morning. Her eyes are heavy and don't want to open. Listening for Adam's regular breathing, she is satisfied that he is asleep. It has been a long and restless night and she does not want to face this new day. The blood transfusions that have required yet another hospital stay run poorly or not at all and cause Adam's temperature to go up in erratic spikes. And his pain has become intractable, requiring the narcotics he has fought off for so long. Adam has been patient and uncomplaining, but scared in the eyes.

Her own fear at the memory opens Marian's eyes. The light is dim yet; it must be early dawn. The crowded room is eerie from the low perspective of the little cot. Books Stephen arranged for his father break the even line of the window. The long banner Bradley printed out on the computer at school hangs crookedly on the wall facing Adam, like a jaunty marathon finish line. It has nurses and red crosses with ghost-buster slashes through them.

In the dim light an object on the nightstand looks like a small skull, but gradually forms before her tired eyes into a furry little gray mouse with felt ears. Melanie had sent it to her daddy, to keep him company in the hospital. Marian squints her eyes to turn the felt ears back into eye sockets and then back again into perky little gray felt mouse-ears. Now the fear is gone.

"Marian?" Adam's voice is soft, groggy.

"I'm here, Adam," she whispers, but her body simply will not respond.

"Is the paper here yet?" It is a simple question, and he says it clearly enough. But it isn't right somehow. What paper? Does he think they are at home? She becomes vaguely frightened. The adrenaline wakes her completely.

"What paper, Adam?" She sits up so she can see his face.

"The paper," he repeats, emphatically. Then he catches her eyes, becomes confused, then laughs softly. "I guess I was dreaming. Dreaming we were waking up at home." He sounds embarrassed.

She reaches out and takes his hand, bulky with paper tape and IV tubing. "It was a long night, Adam. I'm having a little trouble myself. Maybe I'd better go get us some coffee before we embarrass ourselves in front of the staff." She pulls her body up to standing. It feels heavy, uncooperative. But finally goes forward when she forces it, like a resentful soldier. "No pep," she thinks. And then nearly laughs at such a silly little word in the midst of this debacle. Pep. Hardly an antidote for this bone-weariness. Yet what she wouldn't give for just a little of it. Just enough strength to do the basics out of habit once again instead of by sheer force of will.

"Water," Adam says softly.

"You want a drink of water?" Marian heads for the pitcher on the bedside table.

"No. Dreaming water." His voice is thick with the narcotics. "I dreamed I could breathe underwater. I think I can." His voice is earnest as a child's.

Marian cannot think how to respond. He does not seem to expect an answer, and she is too tired to figure it all out. "I'm going to wash my face and start over, Adam. Just take a few minutes. Do you want anything before I go?"

He stares off as if considering the question and turns back to her with a conspicuous pucker for a kiss.

Marian laughs softly and leans over him, holding his face with both hands. "Anything else, Mr. Stauffer?" and kisses him twice.

He shakes his head "no," then holds up an index finger as if to ask her to wait a moment. But the thought leaves him and he shakes his head slowly "no."

She grabs up her overnight bag and goes into the tiny bathroom. In the solitude she remembers her own dream. Misty now, only fragments of it will form before her mind's eye. She remembers walking in the air, high, just out of reach of those who would tug her back down to the ground. What had the rest been? She had been trying to get back . . . oh yes, back to her children. She had left the children in Austin on the way down and she had to get back to them. She seemed to know that something bad was going to happen to them. She had to get back. The panic and necessity had enabled her to simply rise above everyone's heads and set out in long strides. Long, sliding, airy strides back to Austin. To rescue her children. Someone had tried to pull her down, grabbing her heels. She bobbed, but rose again, like a helium balloon. The horror in it had been that she strode and strode, but seemed to make no progress.

She can remember waking with a single thought. What was it? It had slipped away when she turned her focus to Adam's sleepy talk. She had been angry in her dream. Someone, maybe the person who tugged at her heels, told her to just trust God to take care of the children. Yes, that was it. And that was the source of her anger. "I don't trust God," she said to the faceless tormentor in her dream. Resignation she might could muster up. But trust? No, she doesn't think so.

The hospital rumbles into morning. She is glad it isn't a large teaching hospital like the one back home in Chicago. Here the personnel is ninety percent Hispanic, like the local population. Many of the employees don't speak English and she enjoys their lilting chatter. Adam gets along quite well in Spanish, though he doesn't admit it. Says he speaks it freely, not fluently. The hospital menu offers things Adam has to explain to Marian: envueltos, chalupas, fajitas. And always tortillas. Now that the annual influx of retirees—"winter Texans," the locals call them—has left, the hospital census is down and the pace is slower. It is more noticeable that Spanish prevails in the hallways. Marian can never quite shake the feeling that they are traveling in a foreign country.

The hospital personnel here are at the same time less professional and more humane than back home, the doctors dandyish like old-time country doctors, still taking a nurse with them on rounds. The nurses call her "mi 'jita" which, as close as she can get from Adam, means "little daughter."

"Mr. Stauffer," the first nurse calls briskly, entering with medication. Marian recognizes the Spanish inflection—"Estofer"—of Hilda, the daytime medication nurse.

"Good morning, Hilda," Marian comes out of the bathroom and greets her.

"Yes, good morning. Here are Mr. Stauffer's pills." She is shy and kind, with a warm voice.

"Water," Adam begins, and then waves his arm around as if catching flies. The IV tubing restricts him to a purposeless wavering salute. The look in his eyes is so vacant and his response to Hilda is out of character. Marian knows the drugs are bound to affect him, but she is becoming genuinely alarmed now.

"Adam," Marian begins, "it's Hilda. She has your pills."

"I can breathe under water," he tells her. Impossible to tell if he is totally out of it or only teasing.

"Your dream?" Marian asks. When he turns his vacant gaze to her, Marian knows he isn't teasing. "Adam, are you dreaming?" She is frightened now. "Hilda, I think maybe you'd better call a doctor to look at him." The doctor, yes, the hero and the enemy. The "Stockholm Effect." She wants them here even though they are powerless now, puny wizards blowing smoke around the fact of their impotence. Blood, lab tests, X-rays, more blood—smoke, all of it. But she will have them.

Hilda calmly sets her medication tray down and takes Adam's pulse and blood pressure. "Mr. Estofer," she talks to him while she works. "Mr. Estofer, are you feeling better this morning?"

"Yes." His answer is weak, but sure.

"Did you have a bad night?" She talks a little too loud, but her voice is calm, reassuring.

"Yes," his gaze focuses on her face, the expression clearing for a moment. "I dreamed I could breathe underwater."

Hilda traces the plastic tubing from the hanging IV fluids and continues to talk. "Mr. Stauffer, do you know what day it is?"

Adam looks blank for a moment, then turns to her and answers clearly, "If this is Brussels, it must be Wednesday."

"And your name?" Her voice is calm. She has played this game before.

Adam stares out of the window for so long that Marian thinks he has drifted out again. Finally he turns to Hilda and says, "Adam Estofer," echoing her accent softly, the old sly grin replacing the vacant smile.

Marian is so relieved she almost cries. "Adam, you devil. You frightened me." Hilda looks at her, confused. "It's all right, Hilda. He's all right." She still looks uncertain, so Marian continues. "His blood pressure and everything is okay, isn't it?"

"Oh, yes."

"Well, thank you for checking. He's all right now."

"You are sure?"

"Oh, yes. Quite sure." Marian shakes her finger at Adam and frowns.

"Well, then, take these pills, please." Hilda's voice is kind, though humorless. Perhaps she doesn't grasp it entirely.

Adam does as he is told and sinks back into his pillows. "Thanks, Hilda."

Marian closes the door behind the nurse and then sits down,

weak with relief. She can feel her body chemistry change with the sudden reprieve, much like the let-down reflex back when she had nursed the babies. An inexplicable combination of physiology and emotion.

"What time is it, Marian?"

"A little after seven now."

"And what day is it really?" He is upset, she can tell.

"Adam, what's wrong? It really is Wednesday."

"Okay."

"You didn't really know, Adam?"

"Not for sure." He stares out the window. "Is that the freeway?"

"Yes. Expressway 83."

"So which way is north?"

"See that subdivision on the other side of those trees?"

"Yes."

"That's due north."

"Good. Thanks." They stare silently out at the wide curve of freeway lifting over the flat expanse of land, then watch the closer intersection as a yellow school bus disgorges bodies one at a time in an odd peristaltic move of crowded bodies. Finally, Marian forces her attention back to Adam.

"What's the matter, Adam? You seem sad. Are you in pain again?"

"No. No, I'm all right. It's just the dreams."

"Breathing under water?"

"Better than that. I dreamed it healed me. I stayed under the water a long time. Long enough to realize I could breathe there. When I came out I wasn't sick anymore. At first I didn't notice; just thought how clean and fresh I felt. Then I noticed I was strong." Adam waits a moment, runs his hand over the fuzzy halo of regrown hair. "I ran and ran, then stopped and picked up something. I don't know what it was. Something heavy. And I could breathe right. And my hair was right. And I didn't have any tubes hanging on me." His voice sounds angry at that, and he waves his arms around like a manacled prisoner, wrists close together.

"I know, Adam, I know . . ."

"And I didn't have fever, and nothing hurt, and I wasn't sick to my stomach. I looked at my arms and there weren't any bruises or bloody scabs, and I looked in the mirror and there weren't any radiation burns." He keeps his eyes averted from her look, staring intently out the window. "It was just so real, Marian. A technicolor dream. Just so real. You know the kind. More real than the gray world when you do wake up."

"Yes, I know what you mean." She pulls the chair closer to his bed and takes his hand. She wants so much to be strong for him, to give him strength somehow, pass it from her hand to his. But she feels a sinking weakness that takes her away from him and she can only say, "I know."

Adam closes his eyes hard and two tears wind their way down his cheeks, ashen now with his illness and the long night. Hesitant at first, the matching crystal rivulets find their way down through the early-morning stubble, yet to be shaved, then disappear around the edge of his strong jaw. "I don't want to fight anymore, Marian. Not anymore."

"Adam . . ."

"There's worse things than dying, Marian."

They are quiet for several moments, then realize that the door is open. Blake is standing there poised with one hand on the handle, the other holding his working hat. His stooped, lanky frame is highlighted against the brighter hallway.

"Hello, Blake," Marian and Adam say, almost in unison.

Only then does Blake let the heavy door go so it closes in a soft whisper.

"Adam, Marian." He greets them with a curt nod. "The kids had a ride to school with one of Stephen's friends, so I came on into town to pick up some things. Thought I'd see how things are going up here." He shifts from one foot to the other.

"Are the kids all right? They're not giving you any trouble, I hope?" Marian asks.

"No, no. Everything's fine. Doctor said Stephen's collarbone is healing just fine."

She had completely forgotten about Stephen's doctor appointment. "Thanks for taking him, Blake. And for helping Melanie call last night. She was a little lonesome." It is hard for her to talk to Blake past the amenities. He just doesn't respond like most people. Or, more accurately, he often doesn't respond at all. Today, for some reason, he seems positively garrulous.

"Oh, she's all right now. This morning those eggs she's been watchin' hatched. Seven of 'em. Well, six hatched and Melanie drove us all crazy until we helped that seventh one along. I don't like to do that, there's usually somethin wrong with 'em and they end up dyin'. But you know Mellie; she warted us 'til we got 'im out. He's got crookedy feet, all right, just like I warned her."

"Wait, don't tell me. He's her favorite, right?" Adam's voice is stronger now.

"Oh, Lord yes. He's got a name and everything."

Marian busies herself getting a wet washcloth and washing Adam's face, tidying up the cot. She gradually steers Blake closer to the bedside where he stands uncomfortably, staring at the large burgundy splats as the blood drops hit the filter in the tubing right at his eye level. They don't speak for a long while. Adam finally murmurs something about news from the outside world and turns the TV on with the bedside remote. The television's low drone replaces their silence and gives them all somewhere to focus their eyes and attention. A commercial blares out in a higher volume: "The one simple idea that changes peoples' lives."

"I can hardly wait," Adam murmurs sarcastically.

"Daily Fiber Therapy!" the ad concludes, exultantly.

"Daily *what*?" Blake asks, squinting at the set.

"You remember when the 'one simple idea that changes peoples' lives' used to be Jesus Christ, don't you, Dad?"

Marian can tell that Blake doesn't quite get the joke Adam is making, but they both know the moment is special for another reason: it is the first time Adam has ever called Blake "Dad."

"Really," is all Blake says. But his stance is more relaxed, the silence almost companionable. Marian even finally coaxes Blake into a chair.

"Have the doctors been by yet?" Blake asks. Marian shakes her head negatively.

"They haven't even brought Adam's breakfast yet. Can I take you to breakfast down in the cafeteria, Blake? My treat."

"No, thanks, Marian. Shoot, you should see what all Fina made us eat for breakfast. She don't want you comin' back thinkin' those kids lost weight."

It seems odd to Marian that Blake, usually so taciturn, speaks so easily of the children. Does he see Adam in them? She used to look for her own father in them when they were small. Blake is strict with the kids, and no great communicator, but seems to have built a good relationship with them all the same, especially with Stephen. Maybe all his stony silence isn't just adolescence; there might be more of Blake in him than they had realized.

The television returns to the program: a screaming crowd of people dressed in outrageous costumes with banners, all yelling to be picked by the host, who was apparently rewarding them when they had the item he requested of them. They all three stare without comprehension until Adam cuts it off in disgust.

"Monty Hall stumped the crowd when he called for someone with any dignity and self-respect!"

"If you are going to stay a few minutes, Blake, I'll just run down and eat breakfast."

"Go on. I'll stay right here." With that, Blake finally sits back in the chair and looks like he might stay rather than bolt.

Once Marian is gone Blake and Adam are silent again.

"Blake . . . Dad," Adam begins, unsure.

Blake turns to him but docs not speak.

"Thanks for coming. Did you find the papers?"

"Yes. They were right where you said they'd be." Blake lays a brown envelope down on the covers but retrieves it quickly as an aide enters with the breakfast tray.

"I'll go ahead and eat. The papers are mainly for you to look at. I just wanted to be sure we understand each other." The aide lingers only long enough to take the cover off the plate and put a straw in the juice cup. "It's our will, the house papers, my profit-sharing papers, and all our insurance policies." Adam pushes the electric button to bring himself to a sitting position. The new position makes him light-headed and kills his desire to eat or drink anything at all. He forces himself to at least try a little, so Marian won't make a fuss about it when she comes back.

Blake makes a motion as if to put the heavy envelope back on the bed. "Adam . . ."

"I know. But I need you to help me. I want you to promise you'll help Marian with all this . . . later." Their silence is deafening. The hospital walls sigh with the oxygen and suction and tales told by the suffering ghosts who lived there. The sounds of crashing stainless steel and rubber wheels from the hallway crescendo steadily.

"Let me help you with that," Blake offers as he opens the little milk carton and the plastic bag of utensils.

"I just can't. Please, do me a favor. Do us all a favor," he adds with a wink. "Put this back on the big cart in the hallway before Marian gets back to inventory it. There's no way I can eat this morning. I'll just keep this little cup of grape juice and nurse it along."

"All right, son." No argument. Only the same stiff determination with which Blake does everything. But the "son" is new.

"It's complicated, you know," Adam says when Blake returns. "Dying. I myself would like to be put in a hole in the ground where I could at least have the decency to rot eventually. Or a pine box, which couldn't prevent it long. But I know that will never happen. Too simple. And I don't want Marian to be left with all those decisions. I really don't want to be displayed in a fancy bronze casket with all the trimmings, but maybe it will help Marian and the kids somehow to do it up right. Anyway, I've got my burial instructions and the company's burial insurance policy in there. Find 'em? I want you to take all that down to Klipper's funeral parlor—

because I love their name—and draw up one of those pre-death arrangements, or whatever they're called." Pre-nuptial, pre-death. They've got advanced planning for everything but birth. He'll have to put Bradley onto that; if he can be first on the market with a "pre-birth" arrangement the legal world will never be the same.

"Here it is," Blake announces. He hands the stapled papers to Adam to confirm.

"Yes, that's the set to go to Klipper's. The only other thing they'll need is a deposit, so I want to sign a check now to send with you."

"When my father died," Blake begins while shuffling through Adam's papers, "I came in from work to find him laid out on the dining table, only the local ranchers and wetbacks for mourners." Blake sounds distant, seems to have no idea of the inappropriateness of his comment.

"Promise you'll put me in a clean suit and it's a deal."

Blake lets Adam's black humor go by, like he does almost all humor. "Funny" just doesn't register with him, it seems. All business. Always. He locates Adam's checkbook and a pen and Adam signs a shaky signature at the bottom, leaving the rest blank.

"That's that," Adam sighs, dropping back into his pillows. He is exhausted, but determined to finish. There are so few opportunities away from Marian and she will not discuss these details. "Just look through the rest and see if there's anything you don't understand." He has never noticed Blake's reading glasses before. His eyes swim large and luminous behind them where they perch crooked on his strong nose. Surprising that he never noticed Blake needed them before. Adam enjoys watching his father's familiar face in this new light.

With few questions Blake finishes going through the papers and gathers them up again into the brown envelope, anonymous, inconspicuous. Marian hadn't even noticed that he had it.

"One thing, Adam. Son." Blake looks unsure, staring out the window, standing, then sitting again. Finally, he stands and holds his own left hand out in front of them both for a moment. "My ring. That is, the wedding ring your momma gave me." He twists the slender gold band off and holds it out in the palm of his right hand. "I always meant for you to have it. Would you take it now? A little earlier than I'd planned . . ." He doesn't know what to say, or, once started, where to end.

Adam takes the ring from him like it is a tiny gem and holds it up to the light. The engraved initials inside are long since worn flat, the outer detailing dulled. But Adam remembers it exactly from the years of seeing it there on his father's hand. Glinting in the sun while he worked on the old tractor, mellow glow on his hand on the steering wheel of the old pickup truck, click, click, click when he turned the hard plastic wheel to take a corner. Meant for him when Blake passed away in a satisfied old age. Here a few years early in his own hand, anticipating his own untimely demise. He slips it on the ring finger of his right hand, a dusky blue color now, thin and trembling. A perfect fit.

17

April 15

I don't think we're in Kansas any more, Toto. Back in the hospital again, little bags of red, yellow and clear liquids flowing into my veins. I fantasize that the prim nurses hold the tubing connection before me for a moment before they hook it up and I sniff it carefully, as if approving a fine wine before dinner.

April 16

"We're all in this alone."—Lily Tomlin

"I like life. It's something to do."—Ronnie Shakes

April 17

Little crippled men strain at the theoretical gnats of the universe while things go on right here in South Texas that even Ripley wouldn't believe. I remember the bright tinsel that I called "happiness," and know it is gone forever. I sometimes mourn for it, knowing I am doomed to live out my days without its bright rattle. But I must say, I am not left empty-handed. No, there is a deep, burnished glow of hope, golden before me all the time. It isn't fun, like the tinsel brightness was, but it is a comfort. Hope for what, I wonder?

April 18

7% of Americans eat at McDonald's every day. Imagine.

The doctors ask to try one more treatment. No. What thou doest, do quickly.

April 19

I can no longer see past the pillar I stand behind—my own last day. Any other business I had here shrinks away into tiny dots on the horizon. It is all finished now. And now that it is finished, I am so light that it takes an effort to hold myself to the earth. Light because the meaning that my life has had is apparent now; I do not have to earn it, do anything to get it. No, it has its own meaning, apart from anything I could do. His strength made perfect in weakness? That ol' cancer did not leave me empty-handed. The pale horse comes and I listen for the hooves even as I fight.

April 20

The narcotics bring only fear as I am pulled under the waves of reality in a slow swoon. There are two shores: one the pain and one the loss of pain, myself stretched taut between them. I refuse the narcotics and the pain becomes my friend, the only reminder of my humanity. It brings cleansing, purging sweats. Awaking soaked with these mysterious springs, I feel renewed, begin to know sleeping from waking. Sleep, with its hungry dreams, begins to take on a shape, a life of its own.

April 21

The dreams have become more real than my life, or the dim shadow left of it. Some are simple: I see hidden things so clearly; I can breathe under water. Some are complex dramas behind a veil: I strive for things that my soul yearns for yet cannot comprehend. Ten dreams, twenty, I don't know . . . My body and my soul no longer want the same thing and I begin to groom one instead of the other. Waking is forgetting now, dreaming is remembering.

April 22

In my dream there are people all around. Silent smiling crowds of the living and the dead. And always my mother, ageless, stars in her hair. I surrender to their silent swirl, a floating, effortless ballet. I thrill to the sound of my own name as it fills the mouth of God. Spoken clean and new like that it sounds like a new name. And I search the pockets of memory for His name, to answer back: "THE LORD IS MY SHEPHERD . . ."

The veil is torn and I am born. Again. Born again. I chant myself awake with it now and do not forget. This last, this best—the twenty-third is it?—dream is my life.

YEA, THOUGH I WALK THROUGH THE VALLEY OF THE SHADOW OF DEATH . . . Now, like the smiling speechless swirl before me, I realize who I am, that I have not known myself before. THY ROD AND THY STAFF THEY COMFORT ME. It comforts me to see them there where they have always been; like my own bed at home comforted me. It comforts me to know that I am not alone in that dark, narrow valley between the living and the dead; that every tiny light from childhood until this day is gathered into a place that waits for me. Even the old, worn words comfort me . . . I WILL DWELL IN THE HOUSE OF THE LORD FOREVER.

18

The dying was easy, Marian thinks, compared to the long road getting there. From the "last, best dream" of his last journal entry, Adam slipped into ten days of semicoma and then, Friday evening, the final goodbye. At that last, gentle moment Blake had only to step into the hallway and remind the rushing nurses, "no code."

Now it is Saturday night, more than twenty-four hours later, and Marian still has not slept. Even after the incredible drudgery of Adam's last hours, the wrenching decisions, and the long procession of callers, she cannot rest, but only sits in the kitchen listening to the settling noises of the household. She has thought more than once of taking a sleeping pill, but knows that is only a trick of mirrors. There is something in her spirit that will sustain her. Something that will be nourished by the children, their friends, Blake and Fina. For so long she had thought that Adam was her strength, that he had given her the power to resist the tiny capsules of concentrated "help" that she knew she must resist. Now she finds she has her own strength. And she has a new wisdom that reminds her to nourish it.

Blake is out on the back porch seeking comfort in a radio farm report; Marian can hear the monotonous alien words from the local extension agent about "disease pressure" and downy mildew on onions due to heavier rains. The children have gone off to bed. Only now does Marian remember Melanie's parting reminder to come and tuck her in. It is the one thing that could have forced her to her feet again.

The old linoleum floor feels cool and clean under her swollen feet as she makes her way back to the little bedroom that she and Adam have shared for the last several months. Where their daughter lies sleeping now.

The rented hospital bed has already been picked up, the oxygen paraphernalia returned, the scattered debris of the sickroom all put away. The tiny bedroom is nearly like it was when they arrived here a few short months—a lifetime—ago. Melanie is asleep on the cot that Marian has used the last few weeks.

Marian smooths back Melanie's wispy bangs, then leans over to kiss her innocent round forehead. The covers are pulled neatly up to her chin so Marian only touches them lightly and kneels to offer her baby the nightly comfort of her presence. Melanie's eyes open briefly.

"Still awake, baby?"

She only nods; then her eyes close heavily once again.

Marian tucks the covers in around her curled form.

"Daddy tucked me in." It is barely a whisper mixed in with a sleepy sigh.

Marian catches her breath, holds her hand suspended just above the covers. But already she can tell that Melanie is snuggled deeply into sleep.

Marian can hear the distant murmur of the boys' voices out on the sleeping porch, then the silly staccato voices of the tiny television they have taken out there. With no cable and only two snowy local channels, she knows they won't watch long. She hears Blake come in from outside, rattle around a minute in the kitchen, and shuffle off to his own room on the other side of the living room. The empty night presses in about her and the sounds become indistinct, then deaden and disappear, as if muted by falling snow.

Still she sits in staring, dry-eyed silence, perched at the foot of the double bed, barefoot but still dressed. She knows it must be after eleven by now, probably nearly midnight, but she cannot make her mind quit racing or her body do her will. The night air through the open window is warm already in April, but the oppressive humidity has lifted with a weak cool front that came through in the early morning. She thinks how Adam loved the brisk new air after a front.

Finally she rouses herself and slips into the living room. It is full of the ticking, creaking mustiness of old houses and lit by the cinematic glow of the full moon flooding it from a cloudless sky. Pausing, she thinks how like Margaret the old-fashioned little room still is, all these years later. As if Margaret's sweet ghost inhabits it still and keeps it to suit herself. The same lemon oil polish on the furniture permeates the air, the same braided rugs muffle Marian's footstep, though they are flat and threadbare now with age. All just as Margaret left it.

The door to the porch sticks, so she has to force it, groaning, past the warped threshold. Stephen and Bradley both turn to her.

"Tryin' to sneak up on us again, Mom?" Bradley deadpans as he makes the "okay" sign with his hand.

Stephen turns back silently to the television. Then, as if in afterthought, says "Hi, Mom."

"You boys okay? Need anything before I turn in? It's getting late . . ."

"Well, I could use a sandwich," Bradley begins.

"Shut up," Stephen drawls, without rancor, as his long arm lazily swats Bradley. His eyes never leave the television.

"Mom!" Bradley sits upright and points accusingly at Stephen, who is already a statue again. "You saw that, Mom!" Then he lies back down in disgust. "Sibling abuse . . ."

"It is a little late to be disturbing Granddad ratting around in the kitchen, Bradley." It feels so good to go through all these old familiar motions and she is thankful to Bradley for being just like he always is.

"Gah . . . abused and starving too. Gah . . ." He shakes his head in mock disbelief.

Stephen's eyes are closed now and she can tell the television isn't offering enough to keep them up much longer.

Marian pauses a moment and watches them in the eerie blue glow from the television, then Bradley sits up and turns it off, leaving them in only the washed-out gray incandescence of the moonlight. She closes her eyes to adjust to the dimmer light. When she opens them again Bradley is watching her.

"We're okay, Mom." His eyes are shining.

"Yes." Still she lingers.

"Good night, Mom," Stephen adds in a sleepy whisper.

"Good night, son."

The velvet night engulfs them quickly here on the sleeping porch, where three sides open out into the night with only screen and metal exterior louvers for walls. Distant sounds— road noise, insects—float in close and merge with the nearby jingle of Sorry's collar and tags. There is a soft swish like a pine forest as the breeze pushes into the fine mesh of the screen.

"Too much air, boys? Should I close some of the louvers?"

"We like it," they say in unison.

She feels a small gust press through the screen and envelop her in a humid embrace. Tomorrow will be warm and humid again, she can tell. The breeze eddies in invisible waves, then settles back into stillness. For a second, she is afraid. Looking around quickly she identifies the shadows, hugging her arms to herself. Then chides herself for being silly and turns to go.

She touches her fingers to her lips to blow the boys a silent kiss and steps back over the threshold, holding the door ajar a minute in indecision, then finally leaning heavily into it to push it closed. A last puff of breeze squeezes through with her and swirls the musty air of the living room. She makes her way over to the bedroom, outlined in soft lamplight.

She begins again to think about the countless arrangements, the minister's visit, the planes to meet, and knows she will not sleep again this night. Her body is exhausted but her mind still races with perverse energy. She will do what she can, will get her gown on anyway, go through the motions. Maybe the routine, the force of habit, will bring peace. Quietly, she moves about the dim room, careful not to disturb Adam . . .

In the split millisecond before the realization that she will never disturb Adam again, she looks up to see him standing there at the door to the bedroom, chuckling to himself and rubbing one hand through his rumpled hair. Yes, his full shock of unruly sandy hair like it always was before he got sick. Before he had chemo. Before he died.

She blinks her eyes and he is gone. She knows it is only the force of memory and habit that conjured him there. Her exhaustion; her longing. She knows she will never see Adam again, or even his smiling apparition. He is gone forever. The last puff of the swirling breeze that had followed her into the room dies in the stale air.

"Stay." She whispers, knowing it cannot be.

The warm reality of the little bedroom reclaims her weary senses: the lamplight, Melanie's soft, regular breathing, and the gentle click of the clock radio at the bedside. Marian pulls the night in close about her like a shawl, turning off the little lamp and dropping to her knees beside Melanie's cot. She lays her hand on Melanie's back and her head down at the edge of the cot. Like she used to do when the children were younger and ill. And she thinks about the fevers, the operations, Stephen's broken collarbone even now, and sees them on a littered highway off into the future for the rest of her life and she is sure she cannot do it without Adam, cannot do it alone.

Then the breeze sweeps in past the mesh of screen once again and lifts her and whispers to her until the fear leaves. A bone-crushing fatigue overcomes her and she dozes. Or only closes her mind to the realities around her. And, for a moment, the room is filled with the same peace it had when Adam was in it with her. She opens her eyes and watches Melanie's glowing face a moment, then lets the leaden lids drop again.

"Isn't she sweet," she thinks. Then, "Adam, isn't she perfect?" And Melanie stirs, and the breeze answers with a soft stirring of its own.

"Adam, you were so brave. Always so good and patient and funny and then, at the last, so brave."

The room swells with her happiness.

"And so hot."

She laughs softly and Melanie smiles in return, still sound asleep. The air, at first heavy with ubiquitous suffering and loneliness, is now thick with grace. Adam himself, and Adam's God, smile and fill her with peace. How can she feel so hopeful, so safe after her hope and safety have been taken from her? Is it possible that there is a place where all the things she loves are held in safety? She imagines a life without sorrow, where children do not break their bones, husbands do not die of cancer.

But the hope is shy, not tame, and leaves her too soon. Why is life taken away too soon?

A puff of air swishes in through the screen and sighs.

"Adam," she whispers, because she is shy of Adam's God.

The barest gust runs its finger down her cheek and loosens a strand of hair. And Marian's exhausted heart is at peace.

Tomorrow those who had loved Adam will gather at his boyhood home. The next day they will take his ravaged body to honor in a church service and then to rest eternally in Roselawn Cemetery. Adam himself had selected the song, a favorite of Margaret's. They will sing it, all together, from the hymnbooks: "WHEN PEACE LIKE A RIVER ATTENDETH MY WAY . . ."

197

It was true; there was peace here. Melanie's soft breathing and the warm night air and Adam's sweet essence.

"WHEN SORROWS LIKE SEA BILLOWS ROLL . . ."

Always there is sorrow. She notices now for the first time that her face is wet with tears.

"WHATEVER MY LOT, THOU HAST TAUGHT ME TO SAY . . ."

She will sing, she and her children, and Blake, and the people whose lives have been woven into their own.

"IT IS WELL, IT IS WELL WITH MY SOUL."

19

Nearly two weeks later, Marian sits alone on the front steps of the old farmhouse reading Adam's journal. She cries freely, unabashedly. There is only Fina to see and Fina cries a steady flow of her own.

The children are in school and Blake is in the fields. Marian has a stack of paperwork on her lap, meaning to attack the ever-escalating pile of bills and forms but sitting reading Adam's journal instead. She thinks there must be an end, a bottom to this well of sorrow, if she can ride rough and wide-eyed over every bruise, every painful detail. She will learn to be comfortable in this saddle, on this wild horse, this bucking, then prancing, then gently loping animal, all blood and sweat and bone. This life. This new life.

She gets out the letter she has been writing to Jessie for days now and leaves it laid out on her lap. The lethargy cannot be only the warm May morning; she must be reluctant still to talk about this new world without Adam.

Off against the distant flat horizon she can see Raul and

the boys moving cattle up to the shed to be sprayed. The ever-present insects sing to her as if it were the dead of summer and the humidity already begins to make the heat oppressive. She becomes aware of tiny flecks of black cinders floating in the air and landing around her. Idly she flicks one from her skirt. Blake says they come from the burning sugar cane fields. None of the elaborate farm machinery is capable of handling so much dead, dried stalk, so the fields must be burned before the cane can be harvested.

Marian looks over her letter to Jessie one last time:

Dear Jessie,

Thank you again for all your help during this terrible year and for coming all this way for the funeral. I never had the time to think about "afterward"; don't think I thought there would be an afterward. I was glad we were here because it was what Adam wanted, but it seemed so strange to be so far from home during the last days of his struggle.

The children are doing well; just a week or so of school, then we'll all be home. Actually, Stephen seems to want to stay here with Blake, if you can imagine—that still has to be talked out. They talk like big-time cattle ranchers; something about building up a herd of Santa Gertrudis. It must be getting serious, because they never talk directly to me about it, but even I can tell you that Santa Gertrudis is ⅜ Brahma and ⅝ Milking Shorthorn, which makes them more heat and insect tolerant than other breeds. Lord, I've got to get back to the museum and get some culture before I turn into a rancher woman. Bradley is "chompin' at the bit" and Melanie's ready to get home and organize the neighborhood again. Plantation life here is gracious, but, like Adam always said, I'll start to apologize for being Anglo. "The land of noblesse oblige" he always called it. Look for us in two weeks; and check on my mother a time or two if you could, please.

I'm so glad Adam worked things out with his father. Blake's really been good to all of us; no sign of the condemnation Adam always seemed to sense from him. He's had the boys going to Sunday school and church; Stephen seems to actually enjoy it and Bradley says that's where all the awesome girls are. He says he's "going around" with one—I forget her name—but that I shouldn't worry, that "going around" is not a verb!

We visit Adam's grave every day. I'm beginning to feel comfortable seeing my own empty plot there next to his freshly turned one. They'll set the marker tomorrow; just like Margaret's and the babies', plain, upright, "I am the resurrection and the life . . ." A family reunion. We all have a strange numb peace right now; the memory of Adam's suffering is too fresh to wish him back. The loneliness is subdued, almost tame sometimes, then blown new and raw again with any provocation. Home will be worse, I know; we shared that space so much longer than this one.

Forgive these odd little charred smudges on the paper. They're burning the sugar cane fields miles away and these tiny black flecks land on us like flies. You barely notice them in the air but before you know it everything is coated with their dark smear.

Soon.

Love, M

Jessie had not seen Adam those last days. Marian had told her about them, but there were some things that just wouldn't tell. How Adam had tried to talk to her; had asked her one last time, "Marian, am I hot?" She hadn't quite been able to make out the words until he touched his trembling index finger to his cracked tongue then touched his own chest.

She had assured him that he was, her tears slipping down to the corners of her mouth. She loved him perfectly then: loved the moist, ashen skin, cracked, blue lips, trembling fingers that looked so long now in relation to his thin body. Body and hands by El Greco. Loved the angry stigmata on both hands, hematomas in every shade and stage of healing. She had held his cold hand to her lips and kissed each black reminder of so many transfusions, injections, extractions. The whole dim swirl of fluids, it seemed, balancing out to zero. "The soldier in white," Adam had joked while still able.

The last ten days of his semicoma were an empty vigil, no more writing, no more talking. He woke and turned to her once, near the end, then turned back to his stupor and said, very plainly, "Oh, look!" And on the last day, too weak for days now to even turn over in the bed, had sat bolt upright, eyes bulging as if in awe or terror, and lifted his arms up above his head as a small child does to be picked up. He had lifted his arms as if to be carried. To What? To Whom? Was it another of his dreams? Or that last dying grace as Adam was lifted out of that broken shell and carried away? Her Adam, long since acquainted with grief, gone now where she could not follow.

Marian finds a careful joy in that memory, likes to think of herself like that too, like Adam at the last with his arms raised up. She had lost herself in the memory at the cemetery, sitting between Bradley and Melanie on the bench, holding their hands, Stephen on ahead with Blake. She thinks she may have physically raised her hands with theirs in them before she realized. If they noticed, they said nothing.

"*Señora*," Fina says from the doorway. But it seems to be a gentle sigh of sympathy. By the time Marian turns to her she is gone.

Fina's somber sentimentality still surprises her. Marian only wishes they could communicate better. The lament of her lifetime, it seems.

"He doesn't understand me," Marian remembers wailing to Jessie a few years—a lifetime—ago.

"The fact that you've confused an intelligent man for seventeen years," Jessie had retorted, "says more about you than it does him." Adam never had really understood her, in the way she wanted to be understood; but he had known her like no one else ever had. Known the things she didn't want anyone to know. And now he is gone, her deepest secrets with him. But oh, how she understands him now. Sees him all at once, the bruised reed he was at the end, with his fuzzy halo of hair, the small sensitive boy caught in the tension in his own home, third-generation ripple from the first hard stone that was cast.

Life is oddly the same without Adam. The same details of living, but with a silken tent cast over it. Everything that has been "life" is still there, but in the diffuse light of this billowing, silken canopy. The children are confused, and relieved in a way. She has to admit, each day is easier and each night newly available for sleeping. No new crises wait around every corner. But their rest is not refreshing, tainted as it is by the guilt at their relief. Their loss and grief are a tight bud, yet to fully open.

It is strange how easily one loss melds with the others: her

father receding forever on the misty horizon, her babies rolling mysteriously, happily in her abdomen, the chubby flaxen-
haired angels with the wet kisses the children were as toddlers.
All gone and yet not gone. We mourn the living as well as
the dead. Redeemed, each one, by the only thing that ever
redeems anything—that silvery pale shadow called love. The
tide comes in and goes out and there in the rubble, it is the
only shell with life still in it. Not the dishes she's washed or
the weeds she's pulled or the paychecks she's earned or the
committees she's been on. Just the love that caused the clutter
to fall in just the way that it did. "There's only ever been one
story," Adam always says . . . said.

The hackberry and mesquite trees around the ranch still
wear the new green finery of spring. As Marian looks out to
the dusty cloud over the moving cattle she hears the busy animal sounds of late spring. Fina's roosters are crowing over
every egg the hens lay, the hens making a curious uproar of
their own with their frantic cackling. She can just make out
that Fina is hunting for stray yard eggs and fixing nests for the
hens that are *culeca*. Marian gathers that it means "setting"
and that Fina will only allow a privileged few that luxury.
Those huge brown eggs with the bright orange yolks are for
Fina's kitchen and she means to have them.

Everyone is busy with animals at this time of year. The goat
Bradley has been alternately chasing and tying since December has been brought up to a makeshift pen by the garage and
has since presented them with twin babies. The long hutch of
rabbits is bustling with its newly quadrupled population as
the tiny quivering noses and still-flat pink velvet ears peek out
to have a first look. The horses and—thank heaven—the dogs

are the only animals that haven't presented them with new family members this spring. Marian thinks of Adam's dogs, Sigmund and Anna, staying with Jessie back home. What will they think when she comes for them without Adam?

Well, they'll think the same things she does: where is that familiar voice, beloved step, even scent? Where? They'll wonder why she is withholding him from them. Blame her, perhaps. She will love them, care for them. Like Adam had. The children will help, of course. They will all help each other. And they will heal. Life will go on, after all. Animals know that. People want to hold on to something from everyone they see pass from this world. And leave something of their own, as a sign they, too, passed this way. But not animals.

She hears the hollow crunch of caliche popping against rubber tires. The friendly fuss the dogs put up tells her it must be Blake, coming home for lunch. The clatter from the kitchen picks up for a moment and then the back door slams. Marian decides not to go in; Blake treats the lunch break as one more chore to be gotten through. Conversation would just be an interruption.

Marian leans her head against the wall behind her chair. The sultry weather makes her sleepy. In fact, she is sleepy all the time, napping throughout the day as if to recover the hours lost during the long slow-motion beginning of this sad year and the wretched ruined nights of its slow-motion end.

She hugs the papers close to her chest so her relaxing grip won't drop them. And dreams. And knows she is dreaming. She hears the phone ringing, distant and sure. It is the hospital, calling to say that Adam is asking for her. But no, she shakes herself awake and her heart turns to lead. It isn't the hospital, isn't Adam. Won't ever be Adam again.

"Marian?" Blake's voice is soft.

"Yes?" She forces herself to alertness.

"You asleep?"

"I think I did doze off a minute."

"Bradley called. Says he'll be late coming home, but he has a ride."

"Is he still on the phone?" She rises slowly.

"No, no. That was all. He just said to tell you, and I wasn't sure where you were." Blake closes the door softly and retreats into the dim interior.

"Thanks." She drops back down into the deep chair, heavy with sleep. And with the dream, receding now, dragging her disappointed heart with it.

She floats in that dreamy state for a long while, but the visions never disperse into the wide pattern of sleep. No, there are too many things to think about, and she goes over them like grocery lists in her mind. Driving all that way home with just the children. Stephen will help with the driving. Even if she lets him stay with Blake, he can drive home with them and fly back. The house will seem so empty; is their security enough? Will they let her have her old job back at the museum? She remembers the bright, clean, cavernous rooms there with a deep satisfaction and surprising longing. She'll offer to sweep out, work for free, anything. Yes, they'll have to take her back.

Then there are the bills, the insurance forms to fill out, the will to probate. No end, seemingly, to the trail of paperwork and decisions. She forces her heavy eyes open and gathers the papers she has clasped to her chest, tapping their bottom edge on her lap to even them up. There is one thing different, she notices, fully awake now, but with the happy hope and mystery of dreams still fresh—she is no longer afraid. She couldn't say when the fear left her, but she can tell that it is gone. There is still the busy sort of worry, and the ever-growing sense of newness. But no fear.

Melanie's black dog Sorry comes up on the porch and noses her elbow in hopes of some attention. A gangly adolescent now, the dog wears a rolled red cloth around his neck that Melanie has fixed for him in lieu of a collar. He whines and turns around in a tight twist and noses her elbow again.

"All right, all right," Marian relents, shifting her papers to her left arm so she can scratch Sorry's ears with her right. He immediately sits and points his nose off toward the horizon with a look of noble bliss. Marian supposes they'll have him in the car going home, too. It's a really bad idea, and will be a problem with Sigmund and Anna. But she doesn't have the heart to tear Melanie away from him after all they've been through together.

"Sorry, old boy, wonder how you'll like city life?" He answers with a high whine and doleful sidelong glance. Marian hates to think of the scene with the other dogs, but it gives her a small rush of pleasure to imagine Melanie's squeal of delight when Marian tells her she can take him with them. Who knows what she'll have to promise Bradley when he hears about it.

Sorry sighs and lies down for yet another nap as Marian turns back to her paperwork. She is more patient now. The bills, the insurance forms, the records, all will come clear, will right themselves as she ponders them with her mind. Other things, she knows, you can only ponder in your heart. Let go, like a baby fallen away from the breast, slack-jawed, arms fallen back in total surrender. Still, she sifts through the facts, hoping to make sense of it all. It has something to do with faith, she thinks. And something to do with children.

ABOUT THE AUTHOR

Kathlyn Whitsitt Egbert received a B.S. in nursing from the University of Texas Medical Branch at Galveston and an M.A. in English from the University of Texas, Pan American. She lives with her husband and two daughters in McAllen, Texas.